TWO ENDS of SLEEP

a novel

LIZARD JONES

PRESS GANG PUBLISHERS / VANCOUVER

Copyright © 1997 Lizard Jones
1 2 3 4   00 99 98 97

All rights reserved. This book may not be reproduced in part or in whole by any means without written permission from the Publisher, except for the use of short passages for review purposes. All correspondence should be addressed to Press Gang Publishers.

The Publisher acknowledges financial assistance from the Canada Council, the Book Publishing Industry Development Program of the Department of Canadian Heritage, and the Cultural Services Branch, Province of British Columbia.

An earlier version of this book won Honourable Mention in the 1995 International 3-Day Novel Competition. An excerpt has appeared in *sub-TERRAIN* (fall/winter 1996).

The epigraph is from "Instructions," from the album *Spine* by Veda Hille © Veda Hille 1996 (SOCAN). Used with permission.

Canadian Cataloguing in Publication Data

Jones, Lizard, 1961-
  Two ends of sleep

  ISBN 0-88974-072-0

  I. Title.
PS8569.O5245T86 1997   C813'.54   C97-910060-7
PR9199.3.J636T86 1997

Edited by Nancy Pollak
Design by Val Speidel
Cover art ©1997 by Suzo Hickey, *Eating Bread and Honey*
Author photo by Suzo Hickey
Typeset in Fournier
Printed by Best Book Manufacturers
Printed on acid-free paper ∞
Printed and bound in Canada

Press Gang Publishers
101 - 225 East 17th Avenue
Vancouver, B.C. V5V 1A6 Canada
Tel: 604-876-7787   Fax: 604-876-7892

For Susan Whitehouse, who I never got to meet.

17. Remember to surface.
18. Endeavour to dive.

—Veda Hille, "Instructions"

The phone rang at about eleven in the morning. Rusty lay there, listening. One, two. Should she answer? After four rings the voice mail kicked in. The phone went silent.

But it had done its job. Rusty was awake now. Kind of.

Her body was inert, flattened like melting wax on the bed.

Open, close, open went her eyes. The curtain beside her was being pulled out the open part of the window. The aloe vera plant continued to struggle on the sill. A desert plant, who could tell when it needed watering?

Outside the window the sky was blue, with curved repeating clouds that Rusty would have been able to identify if she hadn't lost her *Field Guide to North American Weather*. The clouds had a great name like "trout skin" or "flounder back." Something fishy. She didn't remember.

Inside, the walls had not changed: two yellow surfaces that showed red underneath, one blue, and one white where Janet had become bored with painting. In one corner, the yellow met the blue, which marked its territory with a wavy fading edge. Rusty liked to lie in bed and trace the wavy line with her eyes till it disappeared behind the desk. She did that now.

Two kinds of people had walls like this—painters, and people who pretended they lived in old European villas.

She picked up a magazine from beside the bed and read

about the horrible parenting skills of some famous poet till she fell asleep again.

Later, she listened to the phone message. Janet. She went downstairs to her mailbox to get her cheque. She ate some lunch. She listened to the radio.

The phone rang again. It was Janet.

"Hi, I called you before but I guess you weren't up."

"No."

"So what have you been doing?"

"Nothing."

"Come on, Rusty, really."

"Nothing. I check my mail, I answer the phone, I listen to the CBC."

"Did you get your cheque today?"

"Yes."

"Well, that's good. You're not supposed to do anything. Have a nap. I'll be home later."

Now Rusty was suspended, waiting for Janet even though she would have nothing to say when she arrived. Every day the same.

Rusty was tired. She went back to bed. Woke up for some dinner, which she found in the freezer, went back to bed.

Janet got home late. She tried to wake Rusty up. Rusty rolled over, cranky.

Rusty was a horse. She was a palomino with the softest coat imaginable and had never felt the touch of human hands. Rusty's best friend was Scout, a black mare with a white star on her forehead. They galloped free across the foothills with Chief and Velvet and Silver and Shadow.

Sometimes one of them was tamed by a young girl who met them in the grass and talked them into horse bondage—bridle, reins, saddle, crop.

This was when Rusty was eleven. They all said they would only use horse names from now on, and Rusty did. She refused to come in when her mother called her by her old name, Julia. She stayed right where she was in the yard, prancing and shaking her mane.

Then she had to tell people, one by one. "My name is Rusty."

"Isn't that a man's name?"

"R-u-s-t-y. Like the chicken."

"Chicken?"

"Like the chicken on 'The Friendly Giant.' "

"It's not a chicken, it's a rooster, and it's a man's name."

"It's my name."

"At least you didn't name yourself after the giraffe," said her mother. "Jerome."

"I'm not named after the rooster. I am named after a horse."

Rusty had been Rusty for as long as she could remember. She was a lesbian, so no one said anything about her name. She sat in the circle when they introduced themselves: Moonbeam, Sequoia, Ann-archy, Brie. Rusty. I'm not trippy like you, she thought. I'm a horse. If I had named myself only a few years earlier I might have been Betty (Rubble). Or Pebbles or Bam Bam, whichever one was the girl.

Scout, Chief, Velvet, Silver and Shadow weren't like Rusty. They weren't lesbians. They didn't have horse names anymore, either. They weren't horses. Unless maybe they were the kind of horses you see on trail rides, eyes focused on the rump ahead, skin twitching restlessly from stem to stern, breath expelled in a heavy sigh as a rider is lifted on or off.

Rusty's name was the least of their differences when they saw each other, which was never.

Rusty had come to Vancouver for one of the usual reasons: to escape winter. She was escaping the cold and refused to acknowledge the rain. For years she lived here, and for years she had no rain coat, no boots. In winter she walked through the downpours, below the thick dead skies, in wet socks.

Janet lived in Vancouver for the girls. Or so she said.

" 'For the girl' would be more accurate," said Rusty. Rusty was Janet's first and, so far, only lesbian relationship.

"I would never turn anyone down," insisted Janet, "but it never comes up." Which was fine with Rusty, really, though she liked to think of them, Rusty and Janet, as wild and uninhibited and non-monogamous.

"Go right ahead," said Janet.

Rusty had to acknowledge that non-monogamy was different in principle than it was in practice. For one thing, she was not 100 percent sure she could trust her own reactions if Janet did find another, additional, extra girl. With her last girlfriend, well, Rusty hadn't exactly behaved admirably in the non-monogamy department. She had, in fact, gone so far as to call the Other Woman and suggest she not attend certain events. Was this an inadequacy in Rusty's personality? Or was her last girlfriend a cad? Cad, chose Rusty every time, but secretly she wondered.

More importantly, Rusty had no idea how to pick anyone up. She thought it was a bit of a miracle that she had been successful with Janet and figured she might as well quit while she was ahead.

Love is telescopic, the first days huge and detailed, the weeks, months, years later collapsing on themselves. At dinner parties Rusty and her friends liked to relive the charged beginnings, the who-would-have-thoughts. The stories became mythic, familiar.

Rusty liked to start the same each time.

"We met over politics. Can you believe it?" Yes, nodded her friends, remembering Rusty in her late twenties, willing to take on all comers on any issue. Politics had finally made the world make sense and Rusty had been entranced. The resistance of the disadvantaged was not an abstract concept, it was an animal inside her. It was a gut thing that rose in all her thinking, that gathered in her lust. Resistance and empowerment made her smile as she read the books she agreed with, or pieced together her disagreements. Thrilled, she assembled her own arguments, heard her voice lifted in anger at rallies, met other angry women. She couldn't get enough.

Rusty saw a notice in the women's paper *Insister* advertising a meeting to organize against welfare cuts. She wrote the details in her datebook, leaving herself twenty minutes to get there from her AIDS Action Group meeting, hoping to catch the end of a lecture on radical urban planning later, after the welfare meeting.

At the welfare meeting there was this artist who Rusty's friend Lara recognized from some art thing. The artist was early, sitting in a chair near the door while everyone else straggled in. She had short black hair, and her eyebrows joined in the middle. Her neck rose smooth and naked.

"Definitely butch," said Rusty to Lara. Rusty was obsessed with butch/femme classification at the time.

"Explain the dangly earrings," said Lara.

Janet was the artist's name.

Janet had her own reasons for being at the meeting. Her roommate was on welfare and was scared to go to the meeting herself in case her social worker spotted her there.

Not only that. Janet was at the meeting because her mother thought she was wasting her time on art. "All that time and money, and you still won't be able to get a job," her mother said, hectoring. Janet wanted to show her that art was important, though this was a weird way to do so, since Janet's mother thought the welfare rates were too high anyway.

Then came everyone's favourite part of the story. Janet also went to the meeting because a woman in her art history class had joked that half the women involved in feminism were just there to meet girls. Janet thought she might be a lesbian and going to a feminist meeting might be a good idea.

"I was really nervous," said Janet now. Everyone remembered Janet when they first met her, stern and silent. Nervous.

The artist hardly said anything in the meeting, and then she spoke up with an idea to make effigies of the key politicians and leave them on the streets by dumpsters where homeless people lived. Lots of the people at the meeting thought this was a waste of their resources, but Janet was persistent. And funny. She had a shy, self-deprecating way of talking, and a big vocabulary and a sharp wit. Rusty was entranced by her voice and her big hands. Rusty spoke up in defense of the effigy idea and even volunteered to help make them. The meeting grudgingly agreed to provide some money for materials.

Rusty went down one night to Janet's studio in a friend's

garage. It was cold for Vancouver and there was no insulation, so Rusty huddled by the space heater and didn't do much.

The effigies were made entirely of wood.

"Are those supposed to be all wood like that?" asked Rusty.

"Is that a problem?"

"No. I just kind of pictured them, like, paper mâché and cloth and stuff. I know how to do paper mâché," said Rusty.

"Oh."

"I could be more of a help."

"Do you think it's bad that they're wood?" asked Janet.

"No."

"I could change them if it is. Bad, I mean. Or someone else could do them. I already spent the money though."

"I've never done any carpentry," said Rusty.

"That's okay," said Janet. "I can teach you things, if you want."

"I can talk," said Rusty.

"Okay, talk," said Janet.

Rusty talked, first about welfare rights, then about women's rights, then about lesbians. Janet moved around the studio. She wasn't as big as Rusty had remembered. She just had a big presence. She had lots of tools and was meticulous. She held screws and nails easily in her fingers.

The night wore on. The effigies seemed finished, but Janet kept going. She sanded everything.

Sometimes she asked Rusty to hold something while she worked on it. They stood side by side. Rusty kept talking.

"I need a break," said Janet. "What time is it?"

Rusty looked at her watch. Betrayer. 1:00 A.M. She didn't want to go home.

"It's late," she said.

"Maybe it's time to stop," said Janet.

Janet looked at Rusty's shoes. Rusty looked at Janet's hands.

"I'll make tea," said Janet.

Janet didn't want to go either. She was busying herself with the kettle and the cups.

Rusty sipped her tea slowly. No. She raised the cup to her lips and pretended to sip, but she didn't drink. She was waiting for Janet's move.

Janet's tea didn't seem to be going any faster. She wasn't saying anything, either.

"I'm cold," said Rusty in a stroke of genius. Like she hadn't been freezing all night. Janet fell for it.

"Here," she said, and wrapped a blanket around Rusty. "We can share it."

Under the blanket Rusty's courage grew as though in a greenhouse.

"I could kiss you," she said. It sounded so dorky.

"Okay," said Janet. What a real lesbian would say.

I could kiss you Okay I could kiss you Okay: the mantra of everything that followed. The tentative reach under Janet's shirt. Janet's nipples. The sharp angle of the work light on Janet's collarbone. Rusty's own jeans unbuttoned. Hands in wet wet folds. The sudden heat of the studio. The blanket cast off.

Much later Janet told her it was her first time, with a woman anyway. The dangly earrings.

"Other lesbians are a bit more suave than me," said Rusty. I could kiss you.

Everything about Janet's body interested Rusty. She sat dazed on the bus thinking about it. Her own body jumped when she watched movie kisses.

They had sex all the time. They never slept and they didn't

care. Once on a Greyhound bus and another time in an office where Rusty worked, and all night at each other's places, not noticing the time till the sun came up. Janet came out enthusiastically. She read every lesbian publication she could find. She bought a dildo because that seemed to be what modern lesbians were doing. Rusty happily imparted her accumulated sexual theory.

Together they extolled the virtues of lesbian sexual experimentation, reclamation of lesbian sexual history, allowing freedom to include restraint. Specifically, Rusty gazed happily at Janet's cock, amazed at the gender dysphoria, put on the cock herself and fucked Janet. They talked dirty, discussed butch and femme and s/m. And at the end of each discussion . . .

It was a honeymoon.

That wore off. No one fucks all the time after the first year.

Eventually, trying something new becomes a chore. Eventually, you can't believe you're doing that same thing again. Eventually, getting a good night's sleep seems important. No one tells stories about that.

Rusty and Janet were like everyone else. They had fights, usually about money and how to spend it, or about completely stupid things like the value of "The Waltons," or how to fold T-shirts.

Friends stopped saying "Bring your new date," and said "Bring Janet." Even when they didn't, Rusty and Janet showed up together.

Rusty lay in bed staring at her clothes. They were in a heap, the heap was bigger than the basket and the basket was big. Maybe she should stay in bed on this day, laundry day.

Yesterday had also been laundry day and she had stayed in bed with no bad consequences, unless the heap was a bad consequence. Anyway, the heap was exactly the same size today and would only be marginally bigger tomorrow. If she stayed in bed forever she didn't need to do laundry at all, actually. She would never wear clothes again and Janet would change the sheets because they bugged her when they were dirty.

Her contingency plan would be to buy new underwear and socks when she absolutely had to go out, say, to see her worker or something.

Phew, one problem solved for her lifetime.

I should advertise my services, thought Rusty. Consult a University Graduate: Major Housekeeping Issues Resolved with No Work for You.

After her nap, she noticed that Janet had packed up the heap and strapped it to the cart.

"Do you want me to take this to Laundr-Eeze tomorrow?" Janet asked. She was clearly a saint in the domestic area.

Rusty caved in. "Please. I don't have anything to wear."

A decade of political slogans lived in Rusty's head: However we dress, wherever we go, yes means yes and no means no! *El pueblo unido jamas sera vencido!* Janet had invented one that Rusty happily shouted with their friends: Off our knees and into the trees!

At the end of one of the night-time Gulf War demos, someone handed plastic whistles to Rusty and Janet and Lara.

"Blow the whistle on U.S. aggression!"

"Blow the whistle on militarism!"

"Blow the whistle on the oil companies!"

Soon everyone was whistling. It was an eerie wailing sound.

Some women began to weave a web made of red macramé cord across the street. An activist would stand on the sidewalk and hold one end of cord while the others walked across the street with the unravelling ball. Then someone would stand on the opposite sidewalk as the process was repeated in reverse. Soon there were a lot of people, linked together by the red cord.

"We're going to stop traffic with a Web of Life!" they said. And did. Rusty and Janet and Lara and high school kids and Palestinian solidarity workers and progressive Jewish journalists and a whole bunch of other people swarmed around the Web of Life, blowing their whistles. Cameras were rolling. Spokespeople were speaking.

"I like this, it's an aggressive web," said one woman.

A police car tried to drive through.

No one was ready for this.

The demonstrators ran alongside, about a foot away from the car, and yelled. The cop inside looked scared.

"Blow the whistle on the cop!"

Janet saw her chance. She grabbed the handle of the door. ("The idiot hadn't locked it," she said later.)

The door swung open. The car stopped. Janet stared at the cop and didn't say anything. The cop stared at Janet and looked even more scared. He looked like he thought he was in the wrong place at the wrong time. He looked like the Web of Life offended his love of Smooth Traffic Flow. Janet could have told him that in a battle between cord and car, car would win every time. It was hardly rocket science. Still, he seemed stunned by the power of the web.

The whistling continued, high and piercing.

"What do you think you're doing?" yelled Janet finally. And slammed the door.

They could see the cop assessing Janet's possibly subversive message. By now, his car had been stopped for almost a minute, a long time in the life of a web, in the life of a crowd. Time enough for the crowd to press close in front of the car. There was no going forward. He backed away.

Lara laughed and laughed.

"You showed him, Janet. Boy. *'What do you think you're doing?'*" And then she would laugh again.

Somehow they were all happy. Somehow, even though the war was still going on, and tomorrow they would hear about the Highway of Death or the SCUD missiles or the CNN commentators who thought it was beautiful fireworks. Tonight they confronted a cop. Tonight they owned the streets.

"Blow the whistle on gas guzzlers!" yelled Rusty at a huge car of gawkers crawling by.

"Blow the whistle on the rich!" yelled Lara at a Mercedes Benz.

Later the three of them rode their bikes home to the East End.

"Blow the whistle on unemployment!" yelled Janet.

"Blow the whistle on sexism!"

"Blow the whistle on landlords!"

"Blow the whistle on service charges!"

It was a cool January night that bit at Rusty's face as she rode. Lara's black hair streamed out behind her. Janet raced serpentine down the side streets.

One of them would yell, *What do you think you're doing?* and then all three would blow their whistles.

"Excuse me sir, what do you think you're doing?"

Rusty wanted to ride forever heading home with joy behind her and a green and pink whistle in her mouth.

"There is drudgery in social change," says Billy Bragg.

The steps unfold inexorably, the cards are laid each morning, the order is precise, worn down. First, an issue, then, organizing meetings, then, a demonstration. First poster up at least three weeks before. Always have a leaflet to hand out at the demo. There is always someone who wants to take on everything at once, from the U.S. government to their own landlord. And there's always someone who hopes no one feels bad. There's always someone at the meeting who says, "Let's do something new," and starts on an old old path.

Rusty became one of those people at meetings who said, "We tried that, it won't work."

Not much worked.

And still. On Saturdays they were pulled together like hapless iron filings. Sometimes they marched from beach to beach. Sometimes they gathered on the steps of the old courthouse downtown. It wasn't even the courthouse anymore, just a meaningless building, but no one cared. Some of them stood up and spoke, some of them gave out leaflets.

When had it started to fall apart?

Once, on International Women's Day, Rusty was the emcee. She marched with old friends through the downtown, then cut out early to get to the courthouse and set up for the rally. She had to pee desperately, but it had to wait. She walked briskly, anxiously. She clutched a sweaty handful of leaflets and realized she didn't really care whether any of the shoppers knew about IWD or not. She slalomed through them. She could hear the march a few blocks away, the chants echoing and wavering.

At the courthouse there was no sound system. A woman named Carol came rushing up to Rusty.

"Did you get my message? Is someone picking up the sound system? What are we going to do?"

Rusty remembered the message suddenly. She had done nothing. She had forgotten. No one was picking up the sound system. She had completely forgotten. It had not even crossed her mind.

And then she felt the warm pee trickling down her leg. The heat as her face went red. The fog in her brain as she backed away.

She sat helpless on the toilet in a nearby hotel. It was too late.

Too late to get to the toilet, too late for the rally, too late to change her life.

That was when. That was when.

Usually, at the doctor's office, Rusty was convinced she was dying from an invisible cancerous tumour. Then the doctor would explain the completely common and non-dangerous causes of her distress: strained muscles, sebaceous cysts the doctor could remove in her office, fungus that Rusty could get rid of with shampoo.

So now Rusty told the doctor in a flippant way that she peed her pants, and waited for the boring explanation. But you never can tell. That's why doctors go to school. Instead of her regular reaction, Rusty's doctor asked her a million questions. She put things together that had nothing to do with each other, that happened months apart: Rusty tripping, Rusty sleeping, Rusty seeing double. Then she called a neurologist, and Rusty was diagnosed with Multiple Sclerosis.

"You may be relieved," it said in the pamphlet the neurologist gave her. Yes, Rusty was relieved. Unlike her friends, she could put a name to her weirdnesses.

The two ends of sleep

are the waking states of Multiple Sclerosis. A constant state of dozing off, of just waking up. In between, sleep.

Rusty loves to sleep more than almost anything. No, more than anything. Sometimes she sleeps for the entire night and then the day and then the night. She just wakes up to have a snack.

Rusty can stay up quite late, but then the next day is hell because the sleep rhythms are thrown off.

At 9:00 P.M. she begins to get anxious about getting to bed. By 9:30 she really wants to be there. At 10:00 she starts counting the hours till a normal morning, still ten, okay. By 10:30 it is only nine-and-a-half. By midnight it is eight, the poverty level of sleep. After midnight she wants to cry for the sleep she is not getting.

Sometimes when Rusty and Janet are out together, Rusty says she is tired, and Janet starts preparing to leave, but it takes so long. Rusty stands by, watching the clock, watching the hours of sleep dwindling. Please, she says to herself, *please hurry*.

Rusty knows she will never have a baby because what would she do about the sleep?

Rusty doesn't want a baby anyway, actually.

Rusty knows that before she had MS she fell asleep at least once a day, but now she feels she is performing the act with new skill. Head on the pillow, she burrows her way to the flower behind her eyes, the blue/red/green sideways head she always sees, the soft wet patch below her mouth.

"I know how to fall asleep now," she tells herself. "I am a sleeper."

She does not feel guilty about the sleep. She is proud each time.

At thirty-two, Rusty looked back on her Youth, her Irretrievable Youth. Rusty read somewhere that MS could almost be used as a method of birth control, the patient's sexual desire was so low. It wasn't her desire really, thought Rusty. It was just that, well, she didn't know. She waited for Janet, who was younger (thirty) to come on to her, so she could perform out of a sense of duty. And sometimes she did and sometimes she pretended to be asleep and sometimes she said sweetly, "I'm too tired."

Janet said Rusty was tired all the time and she was tired of always starting things.

"You lie in bed acting like you're already in the grave," said Janet.

"I'll never mountain climb," said Rusty.

"You've never wanted to," said Janet

Janet had dropped out of university because of political principles ("They're just teaching me how to be a member of the managing class and I'm not interested"). She got a job. She worked with another lesbian at a flower shop, as an Assistant Florist. It was BJ's business, Janet helped out. She swept the leaves and stems off the floor. She maintained the buckets of flowers in the fridge. She waited on customers. She loved it.

"I have the perfect job," she said. She never regretted leaving university.

Rusty used to find this attractive in Janet. Now she wanted Janet to finish university. She wanted *someone* to have a career.

"I want you to be somebody," Rusty said.

"I am somebody, asshole."

"Anyway, I have to sleep."

Rusty would storm off to bed and lie awake listening to Janet puttering in the kitchen, or typing on the computer in the next room, or leaving quietly to go to her garage studio. Then Rusty would stare at where yellow met blue, or turn on the light and read.

Janet always respected Rusty's need for sleep, even when it sometimes was a signal that she actually needed comforting. Rusty sent amber signals. It wasn't like in the s/m manuals, where no always meant yes and the safe words were oh-so clear. Rusty would say maybe and mean maybe. It was up to Janet to decide whether to run the light or not. Then Rusty would decide whether to cause the accident. It hadn't always been like this. It was Year Five.

They lived together, two bedrooms, just off the Drive where the lesbians were. All of Rusty's friends strolled on the Drive. Now that she was not working, Rusty ventured out and shopped sometimes. There were lots of small shops and lots of poor people. Rusty among them, she guessed, thinking how she looked one morning wearing her pyjamas, leather jacket, running shoes, when she went to get milk. Pathetic.

The phone rang at eleven in the morning again. Rusty listened.

"Okay, fine," she thought, "I'll get it."

It was Janet.

"Hi."

"Hi. Listen to this. You know how I'm putting you on my extended health plan at work? Well, they'll do same-sex benefits but they won't give you life insurance because you have MS. Can you believe it?"

"Well, yes."

"Aren't you mad?"

"Kind of. I'm a bit sleepy."

"It's ridiculous. You don't have an illness that necessarily affects your life expectancy. If you'd been on the plan before you were diagnosed, they wouldn't be taking it away now. BJ and I are going to fight it."

"Great. I mean, thanks."

Janet exhausted Rusty sometimes. Truth be known, everything exhausted Rusty, but sometimes it was Janet in particular. Just thinking about taking on the insurance company. Better Janet and BJ than her.

She got dressed and went out.

It was a sunny day, crisp. Rusty went to the credit union to cash her cheque, then on to get groceries. She gave some of her welfare money to a woman on a bench outside the post office.

Above the woman's head, on the wall, someone had spray painted "Freedom through action." The m in freedom was on a darker part of the wall, so it read "Freedo through action." Freedodo, thought Rusty, meanly.

On any given day, at least three people would ask her for change. Sometimes she gave money, sometimes not. Today, she liked the imperial majesty of the woman sitting on the bench. Tomorrow she might not. There were so many people depending on her whim. So many more she couldn't see. No one had enough, the Left was dead, women were still being cut up and put in freezers.

The headline in the paper box: "Nabbed in broad daylight."

The headline on the paper by her feet, crumpled: "All fish gone from ocean."

Or something like that.

After the deli, she noticed a woman about to cross at the light. She noticed her at first because the woman was writing down something from a poster on the telephone pole. It had never occurred to Rusty to haul out her datebook on the street and write down information from a poster. She relied on extreme over-postering to engrave the date and time on her memory.

Now the woman was putting her book back in her pack, and crossing.

"Cute," thought Rusty. Where did *that* come from? This was not a characteristic Rusty thought. Certainly not now, in her amber-signal phase.

But cute the woman undeniably was, and Rusty followed her across the street. On the other side of the Drive, the woman turned away. Still Rusty followed. When the woman paused to talk to friends, Rusty looked in the window of the billiard hall. She saw pool tables and lots of teenage boys, coffee cups and crumpled napkins.

Hmmm, she thought, just look at the mess.

She thought she knew how to be a good tail, but obviously not. When she looked back, the women had disappeared. Rusty went home and unpacked her groceries.

Lying in bed for her nap, Rusty thought about The Woman on the Drive. Was The Woman at home in her bed? Rusty thought about watching her. Was she masturbating? She thought about The Woman watching her masturbate. She thought about The Woman seeing her on the Drive, knowing Rusty was following her and then following Rusty home herself, sneaking in the door, standing outside the bedroom, watching Rusty's hand between her thighs.

Rusty fantasized about The Woman. She put The Woman on a beach in Europe with her, making deals with strange men.

Rusty came and then fell asleep.

Rusty didn't like to consider what it might mean that she of the amber signal was having sex in the afternoon, if only with herself. She knew there was a difference between all of the time (never wanting sex) and some of the time (wanting her own skilled hand). But then, Rusty knew a lot of other things she preferred not to think about too.

When Janet came home for dinner, she woke Rusty up. After dinner Rusty returned to bed.

Janet went to a meeting. Rusty slept and dreamt.

Europe on the Beach

Rusty is travelling in Europe by herself. Travelling somewhere by herself. Somewhere strange. She has hooked up with a woman, The Woman on the Drive. The Woman is a sexual partner. She is not altogether nice. There is something too male about her. Attractive, slender, but male. They have been having good sex and now they both need to get home. They don't have any money.

They are at the beach.

Rusty lies in the sun. The Woman is talking to a man down the beach. Rusty feels them looking at her. She feels the hot sun, the rough towel. She feels them looking and is aware of her bathing suit—too small—her breasts, her flat belly. She likes them looking at her, preens a bit, feigns nonchalance, tense all the while with their looking.

The Woman is back. She has made a deal with the man.

The deal involves Rusty.

The deal involves sex.

Rusty is not The Woman's property for her to make deals, but Rusty is interested.

Her cunt is already hot and wet.

The deal is that the man will do what he wants to Rusty. If she has an orgasm, she is his. If she doesn't, Rusty and The Woman will be given enough money to get home.

Rusty is definitely interested. She is hot. She wants The Woman right now, but she is not allowed to come until the deal is transacted at the man's house. The Woman knows where it is.

When they get there the man ties Rusty spread-eagled to the wall, a platform, a table. He attaches clamps to her nipples. She gasps.

People arrive, men, women. All of them are dressed for a party. Rusty is naked, tied. They look at her, they talk to the man in a language she doesn't understand. They talk to The Woman. Some of them are smoking, some of them are masturbating as they look at her. The men are fucking each other, the women are fucking each other. The men are fucking the women.

No one is fucking Rusty.

Finally, the man unties one of her hands.

"You want it, don't you," he says.

"Yes," she says, looking at The Woman.

"Don't come," The Woman mouths the words to her.

But she is rubbing herself in the way only she knows. Everyone knows the deal. The man is leering. The Woman is frowning. But Rusty can't stop. She wants this. She wants the man, more than she wants home, more than The Woman.

When she comes, she sees the man give The Woman her money anyway. The Woman leads Rusty away, her knees weak.

Janet came home with takeout from the Szechuan place: Orange Peel Chicken, Honey Garlic Beef and Szechuan Green Beans. It was Rusty's favourite dinner, and she always felt vaguely decadent eating it, like she shouldn't be allowed to enjoy food so much with so little (zero) effort. Other takeout—pizzas, for instance—did not have this effect.

To top it off they ate in front of the TV. Rusty had never been allowed to eat in front of the TV when she was a child, and then had spent much of her adult life refusing to watch television or even live in a house with one. Now she felt like she had when she first tried recreational drugs: she was headed down the path to personal ruin and wanted to go as far as she could. They were watching a sitcom.

When they finished eating, Rusty snuggled close to Janet on the sofa. She stroked Janet's leg and fondled the back of her neck. She even sucked Janet's ear a bit. Rusty felt her own arousal build. She rubbed the back of her hand against Janet's cheek. But when the show was over, Janet extricated herself from the embrace and began gathering their plates.

"What are you doing?" said Rusty.

"I'm cleaning up. I've got a meeting."

"What?"

"The new art action network. The first meeting is tonight."

Janet scraped food off one plate onto the other and stacked them.

"What?"

"Rusty, you've known about this for ages. They're expecting me." She piled glasses on the plates and went into the kitchen.

"Well why don't you call them and tell them you can't go?" Rusty yelled after her. "People do that all the time."

"No. I made a commitment and I'm sticking to it." Janet came back for the takeout containers.

"What about your commitment to me?" asked Rusty.

"What about it?"

Rusty followed Janet into the kitchen. "I wanted to have sex tonight. I can't believe you want to go to a meeting."

"Don't start guilt-tripping me now." Janet slammed the fridge door. A magnet fell on the floor and broke. They stared at it. Neither of them moved to pick up the pieces.

"I'm not guilt-tripping you. I'm trying to figure out what is so important that you would put it ahead of our relationship."

"You're the one who's always telling me to be more ambitious." Janet tied up her boots. "Think of this meeting as furthering my career or something. I'm actually taking your advice." She put on her jacket.

"I feel like you led me on."

"Oh Christ. That's ridiculous, Rusty, and you know it."

"I'm just left here with the TV."

"Well maybe you'll be lucky and there will be a show on about martyred saints." Janet picked up her keys and datebook, and then she was gone, the door slammed, the windows shaking.

When you have Multiple Sclerosis

you know the bathrooms: in supermarkets, malls, restaurants, clothing stores, banks. In everyone's house, you ask, "Can I use your washroom?"

Rusty has threaded her way through pallets of produce to the door marked "Employees Only," up the stairs to the room of lockers and stalls. She has seen the union bulletin boards, the calendars of women with outsize breasts, the hooks of coats, the makeshift coffee areas, the RSVP lists for staff parties, the signs reading "Wash your hands before returning to work" posted by the Ministry of Health.

Rusty is not afraid to ask anyone. When they say no she goes on down the street, always polite, always desperate. "Hi, is there a washroom here I can use?" When no one says yes, she goes anywhere. On road trips she stops the car by the side of the road. Once in Montreal she used someone's backyard. Once she went behind a parked car on a city street.

It is called "frequency and urgency of urination."

Friend: "Can't you just hold it till we get back?"

Rusty: "No, I cannot." She doesn't want to say she will pee her pants like a puppy. And she will.

Here is what you learn: Always sit on the aisle. Do not drink anything the day of a car trip. Never unpack the car before you go in to pee.

Gauge the level of desperation.

Should I get in line for the toilets now because by the time I am at the front I will have to go?

Rusty reads the graffiti in the stalls. It is remarkably consistent in terms of style and content. Every time she reads something new, she decides to go back to whoever she's with and recite it— and every time she forgets. Then the next time she reads graffiti, she remembers all the previous stalls. It has its own narrative, full and rich. She doesn't think of adding to it. She doesn't even think of anyone ever actually writing it. It is just there.

Here I sit broken hearted

Paid a dime and only farted

Yesterday I took a chance

Saved my dime and shit my pants

Rusty spent some time when she was a girl memorizing this one. A classic. It seemed so hilarious.

Rusty woke early one morning, at ten, so she could be ready for her lunch date with Lara. Lara was taking Rusty out to lunch, which was a big deal for Lara so Rusty figured she had better not be late and probably not be sleepy. She splashed cold water on her face repeatedly. She paced to get her circulation going.

At twelve she headed to the restaurant. The weather was dreary, Rusty's feet were wet. A young man with red dreadlocks was putting up posters on telephone poles. Rusty read one: "NAFTA NAFTA We Don't Hafta." It had a picture of a Mexican worker in a sea of mud. In one of those Free Trade Zones, Rusty guessed. On the other side of the Drive a man in a safety vest was using a paint scraper to take down all the posters that had just gone up. He worked for the city. Rusty felt like she was watching a pair of Sisyphuses.

In the restaurant, Lara was sitting with The Woman.

It never rains but it pours, thought Rusty.

She felt intimately connected with The Woman, having done intimate things with her only a few days before.

"Rusty, this is my friend Dee," said Lara. "I hope you don't mind if she eats with us."

"Not at all," said Rusty. Cute, she thought again, pondering Dee's thin, chapped lips. Rusty had always liked thin lips. Dee's hair was shoulder length, thick and greying.

"Lara tells me you have MS," said Dee.

"Yes."

"My mother has an old friend who has MS, and you know she swears by Tai Chi." She smiled at Lara. "She says it's extended her ability to walk by twenty years."

Rusty knew Dee smiled at Lara because Dee thought since Lara was Asian, she must care about Tai Chi. Rusty knew Lara, though, and she knew that Tai Chi was probably far from her mind. She was probably thinking about guardianship legislation or what to order for lunch.

"Yeah, people seem to be into Tai Chi," said Rusty.

"What are you doing for your healing?"

"For my healing?" Rusty pondered the realization that Dee was losing her cuteness by the second. "I sleep a lot. I always know where the toilet is. I'm on welfare."

"You've got to take care of yourself."

By the nanosecond.

"My girlfriend tries to make enough to keep me in cocaine on the nights I want to go out, ha-ha."

Everyone laughed. Phew, thought Rusty. Let's talk about something else.

"How is Janet?" asked Lara.

"Well, pretty busy with that cocaine thing."

"No, seriously. How's the flower shop?"

"She likes it there. BJ is still really nice, it's still impossible to screw up your politics doing flower arranging, she leaves her work at work."

"Cut flowers waste valuable agricultural land," said Dee.

"Give us bread but give us long-stemmed roses," said Rusty. That was Janet's line.

Of course, Rusty actually wished Janet would get out of the

flower shop thing too. Not because of the agricultural land, but because Janet was too content to stop at Florist, no, Assistant Florist. Rusty wanted Janet to be Lawyer or Administrator or Famous Artist.

When Janet was at university, a professor had recommended that she consider a career in Critical Studies. Rusty had read one of Janet's papers, but she had just read the words. The professor had called it brilliant, which was quite something for an undergraduate paper. Janet could go back and finish her Bachelor's and then a Master's and then a Ph.D. and then be a professor, and Janet could fight battles for same-sex couples in married student housing, while Rusty lay wasting in bed, cheerful and supportive.

Rusty offered to help Janet, because Rusty was an experienced writer even if she didn't know Critical Studies. She had worked for years writing popular legal education materials, and news shorts and feature articles for every little women's rag in the country. She even wrote an arts column for a while. And she had graduated from university before her life had been so cruelly snatched from her.

"Why don't you just go back to school yourself?" said Janet. "You're the one who keeps dreaming about it."

"I couldn't do it."

"If you can help me, you can go yourself."

Ah, Janet. Much nicer and smarter and, frankly, cuter than Dee, who seemed to be a professional of some kind. Rusty missed a lot of the conversation because she kept going to the Ladies' Room.

She used a different stall each time. She worked her way from left to right. In the first stall, black marker had written "I love women," and blue ink had written "So do I, and so does my boyfriend," and scratchmarks had written "Fuck you." In the middle, Rusty learned that "R loves N" and that "T is a bad fuck and sells bad drugs." In the last stall one wall was tile and the other two walls had just been painted.

Rusty read the graffiti and forgot it. She never said anything to Lara and Dee, if they even noticed she was gone three times.

On the Drive a junkie was standing at the bus stop, leaning at an impossible angle. Well, why not? Rusty thought. Maybe she should be a drug addict herself. It was not the prevalence of drug addicts that surprised Rusty, but the lack of them.

Rusty knows a million nurturers,

it turns out. Everyone has an idea about what she should be doing to make herself better. Why does it bug her when they pass on the names of the Tai Chi centres, naturopaths, acupuncturists, home healers? No one is harassing her. Everyone cares. She is glad to have support.

This is a lie. It bugs her a lot sometimes.

Her favourite people are those who want to talk about their illness and compare it to hers. Nabeela has Chronic Fatigue Syndrome. They discuss fatigue until one of them has to sleep.

Suddenly people are very concerned about Rusty in a weird way. "How *are* you?" they say and look into her eyes.

"I *heard*," they say.

"Heard what?" she asked sincerely the first time this happened. Oh, everyone's trying, she knows she knows.

When she got home, she was tired. She walked from room to room, never remembering why she was anywhere. She listened to her messages, but didn't write anything down and then couldn't remember them. She phoned Janet.

"Big J Flowers."

"Hi Janet."

"Hi. How was lunch?"

"Okay. Lara had this friend there, Dee, who I thought was cute and then she bugged me."

"Yeah. She joined my art action group. She's okay. A bit flaky."

Where had Dee come from all of a sudden? Out of nowhere, into Rusty's bed, her lunch dates, her girlfriend's group.

"A bit."

"BJ started your insurance appeal today. I have to tell you what we're doing in my group, though. You know that new centre downtown that's going to have the immigration office?"

"No, but anyway."

"Well, the minister of immigration is coming to open it, and we're going to do a kind of a performance protest when she gets there. Let her know there are Canadians who don't want new laws that are more restrictive. Make *her* feel the heat for a change, instead of just the immigrants."

The performance involved cages, a symbolic march and masks to be laid at the minister's feet. Rusty couldn't keep track, but Janet was elated.

"It's the 'give us bread' part, you know. I do the roses for pay and the bread for free."

Rusty loved Janet. She loved all her contradictions: how she was so shy and so friendly, so serious and so goofy, so boundlessly loving under all her sarcasm. She should have been a mother.

"Like the world needs more selfless mothers," said Janet.

But maybe what Rusty loved was Janet's willingness to get involved in lost causes. It was likely that Rusty was just a lost cause for Janet. Rusty knew that deep down Janet wanted to dump her and get on with her non-sickly life. Janet seemed to have a vision of what she wanted to do and why. It made Rusty jealous. Rusty had no vision for herself. She had plenty of vision for Janet, but Janet was all filled up in the vision department and didn't want Rusty's.

"Every revolution has its artists, its poets," said Janet about her political work. "A painting is as important as a speech."

But Janet didn't make *paintings*. The welfare effigies had been the beginning of a series: huge pieces of art that only worked once, at one demo on one issue. Rusty guessed it was experimental in its own way. The pieces themselves were pretty straightforward: giant puppets, three-dimensional placards in the shape of houses. People always knew exactly what it was about, and Janet was happiest when they laughed or stole sections to take home.

It just didn't seem to fit what, say, Rusty's mother, who had an extensive collection of Monet water lily posters, thought of as art. After Rusty came out to her parents, her mother tried to embrace each new girlfriend, no matter how fleeting. When Rusty told her about Janet, Rusty's mother said she'd like to invest in some of Janet's art. But Janet didn't make art that you could buy.

"I don't make commodities," she said. "But that doesn't mean other people can't. Does your mom want a flower account?"

"The important thing is to say what you need to say, to put yourself down on the side of life," said Janet once, on the phone to someone in her group. Rusty overheard.

Rusty pictured the city worker in the safety vest following behind the symbolic march at the immigration protest, sweeping up masks where they dropped them, methodically dismantling the cages. He was in a union.

After phoning Janet, Rusty lay down for her nap.

First, she thought, I'll come. She tried thinking about The Woman, but the woman was Dee now—and annoying. She tried the Europe on the beach fantasy. Rusty is travelling in Europe by herself. Why Europe? thought Rusty. Too many people in Europe. Okay, travelling somewhere by herself. Somewhere strange. She has hooked up with The Woman. God, not Dee.

Anyway, The Woman is a sexual partner. She is not altogether nice. There is something too male about her. She's a Rasta. Rasta? Maybe not a Rasta, maybe just kind of younger than Rusty, but British. Well, she could be non-anglophone. Maybe in the fantasy, Rusty could be multilingual. Get back on track, her hand said, but she was stuck. The man, what was he wearing? The beach, she thought of Third Beach, where she and Janet had fucked once. Come on, said her hand, but she fell asleep.

Rusty and Janet talked about sex.

Janet was frustrated because they never had sex anymore. Rusty was always too tired.

Rusty was frustrated because Janet always came on to her at midnight, when she should be sleeping. Rusty said she wanted to have more sex, but she didn't really believe herself.

Then she said she just wasn't interested in sex, period. To back this up, she said the world was anti-sex, anti-woman and anti-lesbian, and she didn't see how anyone could have any kind of sex life the way things were going. She said the planet was dying and sex was dying with it. She said death was all anyone seemed to care about, look at that guy who murdered all those girls.

"Well, we should kill *him*," agreed Janet. "You've known this for years, Rusty. Since when does it make you stop having sex?"

Rusty wanted to describe her fantasy about Dee before she knew she was Dee. But she would have to admit that she masturbated even though she never had sex with Janet anymore. She would have to admit that she thought about sex sometimes. She would also have to admit that when she thought about sex it was with another woman, not Janet.

She couldn't think of a frame for the thing with Dee, so she left it stretched in the air. It felt like an affair.

Rusty didn't want to hate everything. Rusty wanted to be back there, in Janet's bed, seeing the grey light start to come in the window, wondering how she could stop, wishing she could just make love all day and all night all the time.

"We need sex therapy," said Janet, "and I have just the thing." She had a copy of a book. *Lesbians Loving*. There were exercises in the book's appendix.

" 'Try feeding each other finger food instead of regular dinner,' " read Janet.

"Next," said Rusty.

" 'Try ironing all her shirts before she comes home from work, and then wearing just a shirt when you go to the door to greet her.' "

"Who wrote this?"

" 'Try telling her how much you love her in song.' "

"What?"

"*Oh, baby baby baby,*" began Janet. "*Really really really, every time I see your boobs, I want to cop a feelie.*"

"That's beautiful and sexy, honey. Let's hop in the sack."

"Classy too," said Janet, sounding like someone on the Home Shopping channel.

"This is not working."

"But I do want you. All the time."

Janet took Rusty slowly, undressing her slowly. Rusty stroked Janet's back, screamed when Janet entered her. She thought of The Woman, Dee, the beach, the man.

"Slow and hard," she said. Janet stroked her slow and hard.

Rusty fucked Janet, lying on top of her. Janet came and then came again. The two of them fell asleep and then woke up later, hours later, to look for covers.

"That wasn't so bad, was it?" said Janet.

No it wasn't at all. Rusty laughed.

"I love you," said Janet.

"I love you," said Rusty. She meant it.

"What was different tonight?" asked Janet.

Nothing. Everything.

"Don't make me tell you," said Rusty.

"Just wondering. I just want to know what worked so I can do it again."

Janet was very excited that they were having sex again. The next night Rusty's vulva felt numb, but she didn't want to say anything so she didn't. Maybe it would change. She didn't know. She kept moving wrong. She watched her own skinny flabby limbs. There was something fascinating about the fact that her body was getting skinnier and skinnier. She could see her ribs. She worried about her muscle tone. Janet came. Rusty flailed around a bit. Janet smiled and held her.

Rusty had never faked it with Janet before, and she knew Janet couldn't tell. She had done it to make Janet happy, but knew this was a bad solution, worse than an outright lie.

Janet didn't notice. Rusty lay awake thinking about that too.

Walls

are a big part of Rusty's life. When you have MS, you never know when you'll run into the one beside you. On bad days it's best to have a grip from the start. Rusty rests her hand on gyproc, smooth and painted, raspy stucco, brick, clapboard, sometimes even glass. She is always thinking of the oily marks her hands will leave. Sometimes she runs into picture frames. Sometimes bulletin boards. Sometimes her hand slides over words, slogans, signs.

Stairs, oh stairs. Rusty grips the banister, leans into the stair, thinks about tipping over, thinks about not tipping over, lifts each foot. With no banister her hand presses five points into the wall. With no wall she toughs it.

When she's not walking, Rusty is always thinking about sitting. Where can she sit? Sometimes it's okay if she can lean on the wall. She looks at the walls for the leaning spots, imagines herself Marlon Brando in *The Wild One*.

"What are you rebelling against?"

"What do you got?"

When it's too much, she sits on the floor, no longer Marlon Brando. Now she is one of those drippy girls in high school who sat on the ground everywhere, cross-legged, feminine, flower children of the mid-seventies.

Rusty may be a femme, but she was never like that.

She wishes she still smoked, just to make it perfectly clear.

Rusty was at the doctor's office, waiting.

She was passing the time in a modern and spiritually advanced way. A way that was "outwardly simple but inwardly rich." She was living in the moment, as the article in front of her advised, sitting "mindfully," which seemed to mean thinking a lot about your situation. This chair is bad and probably leads to lots of chiropractic referrals, she thought. You were supposed to let your mind wander and not "edit" your thoughts.

Once you were an experienced "mindful" sitter and thinker, you could let your actions wander. "Don't edit your impulses," urged the writer, "go with them. If you feel like crossing the street, do it, even if it takes more time to go home that way. Maybe your spirit guide has an adventure in store for you."

Rusty pondered this. She didn't have a lot of impulses and when she did, they often conflicted—the impulse to go to the store and buy junk food, and the impulse to stay home and lie in bed, for instance. She concluded that in the war of unedited impulses, the least impulsive was nearly always the victor.

Her doctor came by with her file and that was that. Her spirit guide would have to wait.

When she got home from the doctor's office, Rusty watched TV. They had cable and a channel-changer, which Rusty used to test her impulses—to surf the endless channels or stay where she was? Maybe her spirit guide had an adventurous show up his/her sleeve. She was watching "Wishbone" when Janet came home.

"Hi, honey," said Janet. "What are you watching?"

" 'Wishbone.' "

"Can you turn it off and come sit in the kitchen?"

"It's almost over. I'll be there in ten minutes."

"It's a show about a dog, for god's sake. I think you can miss the last ten minutes."

"I feel like watching it."

"I feel like talking to my girlfriend."

The article had not explained how to deal with competing impulses when one of them wasn't her own.

"Then wait ten minutes," she said. Even as she spoke, she knew it was the wrong thing. Not capital W Wrong, but wrong for now. The wrong thing. Now they were arguing again. About such a stupid thing. About "Wishbone." The argument was winding higher, out of her reach, about something that she didn't understand. Janet was leading it up up up.

"We hardly get any time together, I come home early so you

won't be asleep and I'm competing with a Jack Russell terrier who dresses up like," she looked at the TV, "like Romeo. This is ridiculous."

"He's cute," said Rusty. She tried to apologize. "Watch with me."

"I don't want to watch 'Wishbone.' "

"Then stop trying to tell me what TV shows to watch." Juliet (a human) was talking to Wishbone as though he was Romeo. It *was* compelling. Rusty *was* watching. She wanted to see the last ten minutes. Eight now. She would argue when it was over.

"I'll argue when it's over," she said.

"I don't want to argue. You can watch whatever TV shows you want. The point is I don't need to lose thirteen dollars an hour to sit in the kitchen while you watch some woman pretend a dog is her boyfriend. See you later. I'm going back to work."

Rusty continued to watch TV as though nothing was wrong.

Janet was cutting her own hair, which she did about every two months. She had been cutting her own hair every two months or so, the same way each time, for more than ten years. She said that was one of the ways she knew she really was a lesbian: she had always had a lesbian haircut.

Rusty disputed the existence of a "lesbian haircut." For one thing, Janet's haircut came from a rather dubious source. She had originally selected it out of *Seventeen* when she was in high school. It was advertised as "gamine." On Janet it couldn't have been too gamine because most of the time no one even thought she was a girl, let alone a perky childlike gamine of a girl. Back then, when someone thought she was a boy, Janet sometimes showed them a Frost 'n' Tip ad with a very femmy model with the same haircut. Rusty seized on the ad: not a lesbian model, ergo not a lesbian haircut.

Also, when Rusty went to the bar she would point to the long, thick, shiny locks, the pert bobs, the neo-hippie ponytails, the dreads and the shaved heads. Rusty would point to the heterosexual farmwomen who had a slightly longer version of Janet's hair.

"My sister has short hair and she's not a lesbian," she said to Janet.

"I'm not saying every woman with short hair is a dyke."

"And look at Lara. She has longer hair than just about anyone and she *is* a lesbian."

"I'm not saying all lesbians have short hair."

"And what about Feather? She blow dries and curls it every day."

"I'm not saying . . ."

"And what about all the lesbians who don't live in this culture? Haircuts might mean something totally different to them."

"Look, I'm just saying that when you have really short hair and you're a woman . . ."

"Lesbians are everywhere, from all classes and races. We are all different, with our own clothes and our own hair styles."

"I know I know, but I do have a lesbian haircut."

"Says who?"

"Say the people on the street who harass me."

"What do they know?"

"Well they know I'm a dyke, for one thing."

For Rusty the politics of haircuts was like looking too closely at a pointillist painting—it all fell apart into tiny pieces. If you followed one argument to its logical conclusion, then everything else got split off into another dot of argument that was right beside another separate dot and then another . . .

The fact remained that, from the outside, Janet's hair did scream "Genderfuck!" and she had suffered the consequences long before coming out. When she was dating Steve (her only boyfriend), the two of them had been assaulted twice by gay bashers who thought Janet was Steve's boyfriend. She had to take a stand by not revealing she was a woman, because that would buy heterosexual privilege. Or did she not reveal it because that might make them madder and rape her? Was she heroic or chicken? Or smart?

Janet's hair-cutting method was precise. She got out the scissors and the clippers. She spread a newspaper over the sink. She took off all her clothes. She cut all her hair just above the knuckles of her fingers laid flat on her head. Then she shaved the sides and the back with clippers.

Rusty's job was to make sure the shaved part tapered neatly into the rest. Then she would take a big brush, the kind used with a dustpan, and sweep the hair off Janet's neck, shoulders, breasts and back.

"Did Steve do this for you?" Rusty asked once.

"I didn't live with him. He thought I went to a barber."

Steve had never known the dark secret of Janet's lesbian hair-styling habits.

Tonight Rusty was sitting on the floor in the hallway, watching Janet wield her tools. The phone rang.

"Hi, Rusty? It's Eleanor."

"Eleanor." Rusty drew a blank. "Sorry, I . . ."

"Scout." The woman whinnied.

"Oh Eleanor! Hi. How are you?"

"I'm doing great, Rusty. How are *you*? I was just back in Lakefield, and I *heard*, from your mother. How are you feeling?"

Why are you phoning me now, after seven years? What were you doing visiting my mother? Rusty contemplated Janet's snipping scissors, her hairy white legs, the swell of her belly. She imagined Eleanor as she had last seen her—coiffed, suited, made-up. She tried to picture Eleanor here, watching Janet. No picture.

"I'm fine, Eleanor, really."

"I know this must be a hard time, Rusty."

"Not really."

"I hope you have all the support you need. I could help out, you know. Like if you need someone to go to the mall with you, you could call me."

I don't go to the mall, thought Rusty.

What was Eleanor hoping for? A cheerful Rusty baking cookies? Eleanor had lots of "support" from her husband Skip, who had once generously offered to fix Rusty up with a male friend. By way of showing off Skip's lack of homophobia, Eleanor had also told Rusty that he was interested in a three-way with another woman. Rusty's "I'll bet he is" seemed to have precipitated the seven-year phone hiatus.

"Yeah, well. Look, I've got to go."

"Who was that?" asked Janet as Rusty swept bits of hair onto the floor and the newspaper.

"Scout. Eleanor."

"What did *she* want? Did she try to tell you you're not really a lesbian again?"

"No, she wants to support me."

"Financially?" Janet sounded sarcastic.

"No. It's my 'condition.' It brings them all out of the woodwork."

"How big of her to finally phone you."

"She didn't have to, you know." Still, Rusty was annoyed.

Sitting at home one day, Rusty heard a chainsaw. When she looked out the window she saw one tree fall down, then another and another. The guy across the street was cutting down all his trees. Rusty had seen him before. He was in his forties and clean cut.

"What are you staring at?" he yelled at a woman stopped on the sidewalk. "This is none of your business."

On the doorstep of the house, a woman and two kids were watching him. Rusty had seen them before too, walking up the street. The kids, one boy and one girl, would run ahead and yell, and their mother would walk slowly behind with a friend. Rusty never knew where they lived. Probably because there were so many trees covering up their house.

Rusty had noticed them because she wondered what it would have been like, to have had a mother who strolled up a street with a friend while she, Rusty, ran ahead. As though children were part of a mother's life. When Rusty's mother entertained a friend, Rusty the child was expected to vacate the premises.

"Vacate the premises!" her mother would say. It was good-natured, but Rusty was expected to obey.

The woman and her kids were staring at the man while he cut down the trees. Rusty guessed it *was* their business.

Rusty could see right into their living room now, which was not nearly as nice a view as the trees had been. The house was pale green. She had never noticed that before.

The thing about Rusty's sleep

is there is no catching up. Even when she has slept a lot, she lives in a movie that is slightly out of focus, where the knobs have been removed from the projector. The movie keeps going on, and Rusty has to get used to the blurring or leave. The waking hours are often difficult and confusing. She has to try to learn to appreciate the washes of colour.

The sleep, on the other hand, the sleep is clear and fluid and forward moving. She slots the radio, or conversations she is overhearing, into the neat logic of her sleepy head. There is room for everything in the dream structure. She tries to bring it into the waking world and the logic collapses, but she can find it again when she sleeps.

One afternoon she dreamt she was visiting her friend Nabeela, who was escaping something. Rusty had to help her even though she didn't know where they were. Rusty was a bit anxious, though not very. Nabeela was calm and happy. It was an adventure. They were in the desert and there were lots of houses, small white houses, each surrounded by a dusty yard. Broken wooden fences lolled everywhere. The sun was hot, and cars and buses were green and yellow and pink and plentiful. Rusty hailed a car, but when they pulled onto the road there was no gas. They stopped at a gas station and Rusty used her Visa card. Rusty and Nabeela stood at the pump together while cars and buses drove by fast, stirring up dust. Behind the gas station was a camel in a small pen, looking morose and skinny. Janet was talking to the camel, and when the car was full the three of them drove off. Janet was behind the wheel. Rusty and Nabeela sang Québécois folk songs to keep her amused. Someone was following them, but it didn't matter. They would catch up, it was inevitable, but for some reason none of them cared very much.

Rusty and Janet's door squeaked. It didn't fit perfectly onto the hinges or something. Rusty and Janet said this was a good thing, they would always be able to hear someone breaking in because the burglar/rapist would not be expecting the squeak.

Relying on the squeak for an alarm was like the other things Rusty did to make herself sleep easy. She liked to sleep in something, at least a T-shirt, so she wouldn't be naked while she battled an invader. She checked all the closets and behind all the doors before she went to bed at night. It was stupid. If there *was* someone hiding, what would they do? Say, "Oh you caught me" and leave?

And if she heard the door squeak in the middle of the night, then what? She would lie there waiting for another sound. That's what she had always done when she *thought* she heard the door squeak. When no burgling sounds ensued, she felt her body relax. And realized she had been paralyzed with fear.

Rusty went out one day for a snack and saw Dee on the Drive with another woman.

"Hi," she said. Without conversation, Dee *was* kind of cute. She had a sharp nose and her skin was taut, almost burnished.

"Rusty, this is Eagle. We're just going for coffee. Wanna come?"

"Okay," said Rusty.

In the coffee shop, Rusty dropped her cup on the way back to their table. Her left hand did that sometimes, just let go. She felt everyone staring. She rested her right hand on a table, went and got another cup, walked fearfully back to Dee and Eagle. No one said anything. She wanted to cry. Dee and Eagle talked.

Rusty watched them from the bottom of an aquarium. Eagle had short hair that she clearly spent a lot of time on. Every strand was topped by a bleached bit and every bleached bit was exactly the same length. The overall effect was a bit like a halo. Over and over again Rusty watched the cup fall from her hand onto the floor.

Eagle was a singer in a band, her own band called Eagle is King. Rusty remembered seeing them play a year ago, before she had been diagnosed, when she used to go out. They weren't bad. Apparently, they had just released a CD. Apparently, Eagle had once met Courtney Love.

"Did you hear that?" said Dee to Rusty. "She met Courtney Love."

"Yeah, she's pretty fucked up, though," said Eagle, straightening her strategically undone overall strap.

Rusty liked Courtney Love even if she was screwing up her life and was a bad mother. Why not, after all, if you're a rock star and can afford a nanny. Why not be a bad mother? No one complained about all the terrible rock star fathers. Rusty wondered why Courtney Love impressed Dee when all she could find to say about Janet was that she was ruining agricultural land. Eagle is King, Rusty is Peasant, she thought bitterly.

In the bathroom, she read "Jesus loves you," "So what?" "Does not," and "He's a two-timer."

She went back to the table. After an appropriate period of time she went home.

At home, she worried about what they thought of her.

In the bedroom, she fantasized that she was in a parking garage, coming home from work, when someone grabbed her. Good, said her busy hand. She thought about parking garages, about being attacked in them. I'm sick, she thought. I'm sick, this is terrifying, it's not a turn-on. She thought about that murderer. God, she thought, no, no, no. No, I do not have rape fantasies of any kind. No.

She thought about Dee and Eagle in the coffee shop. What were they doing now? Maybe they were fucking each other. Maybe Dee's hand reached into Eagle's pants right there at the table. Maybe Eagle gamely kept the conversation going. Maybe now they were at Eagle's place, Dee running her hands over Eagle's waist and arms, Eagle with her head thrown back, raising her hips.

Rusty came.

Parking Lot

Rusty is leaving downtown, in an open-air parking lot, not a parking garage, fumbling for her keys. Someone pushes her against the car. It's a woman, maybe Dee, but she can't see. The woman is behind her, reaching under her skirt.

"Excuse me," the woman says. She has a knife.

Rusty's underpants are soon in shreds on the cement.

Her skirt is up and Rusty can feel the cold air on her cunt, the rough hands on her breasts.

"Please, fuck me," she says.

"I don't even know you," says the woman.

"Oh, please please fuck me."

"Here? So many people will see. Is that what you want? You want people to see?"

"Oh please."

"Tell me. Tell me you want me to fuck you in front of all these people."

"I do I do I do I want you to fuck me in front of everyone. Please."

The woman pushes Rusty over the hood of the car. Rusty feels something hard in her cunt, a dildo. She opens her eyes. A couple sheepishly turn away to their car. The dildo thrusts again and again. When Rusty is exhausted, the woman leaves. Rusty rolls over and masturbates till she comes.

On a wall someone has written "Success is excess." Overhead, the clouds are shifting; white, then grey.

Heat is your enemy.

Rusty loves that. Heat is my enemy, she says to people. I have MS and heat is my enemy. No steam baths, no saunas, no hot baths, no hot showers, no overdressing, no hot cars.

When Rusty has a fever and the heat is in her body, she is paralyzed. It is the worst her MS has been. She cannot walk to the bathroom, she cannot sit up, she pees herself constantly.

When she last visited Montreal, it was fall. She smoked a joint with her friend, and then he left her to wander by herself. It was unseasonably warm, she was overdressed, she had to pee, she lost her sense of direction, she couldn't read. She kept stopping to look at her map, she couldn't decipher it. She couldn't read street signs. She wanted to pee. She was walking down streets of nothingness. It couldn't be the Plateau anymore. Where was she? If she could see anyone she would ask to use their washroom, but there was no one, and she had to pee.

Don't smoke a joint in a strange city if you have MS.

The next day Rusty went up to the Drive to find Dee. She wasn't consciously looking for her. She told herself she wanted a pop, then some bread, then she needed to go down to the cheese store for mozzarella. She looked in the window of the coffee shop. She waited a long time at the light before crossing the Drive.

No Dee.

On the way home, she ignored the feeling of disappointment. She wasn't really disappointed, not really. She didn't even like Dee and she wasn't looking for her, anyway. If she had seen her, she might have just said hi and gone on walking.

"Dee, Shmee," she said to herself. "Big Fucking Dee."

At home, she thought she might phone Dee. Just to say hi, how are things going, hey what's the name of that Tai Chi place? Janet's group phone list was right there beside the phone and there was Dee's name and her number (555-9987), and her address. She lived four blocks from Rusty, closer if you walked along the back lane, which is what Rusty would do when she phoned Dee up at 555-9987 and said hey, what's up, just thought we might have tea. In fifteen minutes Rusty was going to phone Dee at 555-9987. When she had done the dishes Rusty was going to phone Dee at 555-9987. When "Gabereau" was over she was going to phone Dee.

She never did.

When Janet got home Rusty didn't say anything about looking for Dee, or knowing her phone number and where she lived.

"Remember Dee, that woman in your group," she asked Janet, casually. "So, like, does she date that woman Eagle?"

"I don't know. Why?"

"No reason. I just saw them together. I wondered."

"No, I don't think she goes out with anybody. What'd you do today?"

"Nothing. I don't do anything. What did you do?"

"I worked."

"Did you call the university and get an application?"

"No I did not. Why? Because I do not want to go to university again."

"I don't know why you're such an anti-intellectual."

"I think there's a difference between being anti-intellectual and not wanting to go to university to satisfy your girlfriend who thinks her life has stopped and refuses to do anything except nag."

"I don't refuse to do anything. I can't."

"Bullshit."

"You don't understand me."

"That is the first smart thing you have said in a long time."

"You don't fucking care about all those people out there. You just want to fuck and make your stupid art and sell your stupid flowers."

"Bingo."

Later Rusty apologized for belittling Janet's work. And Janet apologized for belittling Rusty's illness.

Rusty stared out the window at the living room across the street, wondering what it would be like to live with a guy who had a chainsaw and knew what was your business and what wasn't. If every human being had a purpose, what was his, she wondered? And if every human being did not have a purpose, which seemed quite probable to her, then she surely did not. Unless her purpose was some puny purpose that helped someone else, someone important, save the world. Like maybe Rusty was going to unwittingly prevent a future Mahatma Gandhi from being run over. Neither of them would ever know.

Maybe, a small voice said, she didn't need a purpose.

Maybe not.

One night Janet suggested that Rusty and she should tell each other sexual fantasies.

"Just so we know we're on the right track if we ever have sex again," she said. Their enthusiastic sexual revival had been short lived. Janet put Rusty's hand on her breast and Rusty left it there, but didn't move.

"You could touch me, you know," said Janet.

"I am," said Rusty.

"Fine," said Janet. Though it didn't seem to be. "Tell me your fantasies."

Rusty thought of a funny story she had heard once, where a woman asked another woman away for the weekend to "read poetry to each other," and the second woman thought she really meant it, and brought a bag of poetry books. Was Rusty being stupid? Was this fantasy thing just foreplay?

"I'll tell you one where I'm in charge," said Rusty. "That's kind of unusual as you know." She cuddled close to Janet and held one of Janet's hands firmly. Keeping the sex away.

"It's kind of a time travel fantasy," she said.

"I don't know if I should hear this," said Janet.

"No, really, I'm at a country house and there's a scientist and she's doing an experiment with time travel—"

"Are you sure this isn't a B-movie? Don't tell me, let me guess, she's German."

"Maybe."

"And she puts you in a machine."

"Kind of."

Janet laughed and laughed. Rusty was hurt.

"You're not supposed to laugh at someone else's fantasies," she said.

"Oh sorry," said Janet. She smiled. "Forget it. Let's just do it instead." She moved her hand along the waistband of Rusty's jeans. It had been foreplay.

"I'm not into it now," said Rusty.

"You're never into it anymore." Janet pulled the hand away. "At least not with me."

"What does that mean?" Did Janet know about Dee?

"Forgive me for pointing this out but I spend a lot of time being rejected by you," said Janet.

"I'm having a hard time. I was into it tonight but you laughed at me." Lying.

"Well so am I having a hard time. It's kind of humiliating. I never know when you want me. Do you want me now?"

"I just want to be alone now. You never let me sleep."

"Fine. I'll leave you alone. Go to sleep."

Rusty heard the door slam. She heard Janet clatter down the front steps. She heard Janet's shoes firm and fast on the sidewalk, fading away.

Shit.

Rusty pretended to be asleep when Janet got back. She heard a vehicle pull up and idle for a long time. She heard Janet say thanks and then laugh. Rusty sat up and looked out the window. Janet was standing at the door of a van, a panel van with a cheesy mural of a fantasy mountain and desert scene on some planet with a lot of moons. Janet laughed again and closed the door of the van. Rusty lay down. She heard Janet's steps on the porch, the squeak of the front door. She heard the van pull away from the curb.

She listened while Janet made herself tea in the kitchen. It was two in the morning. Janet put on music, low. She must be drinking her tea out there. Rusty could get up and talk to her. About what. She heard Janet walk to the kitchen, the muted clang of the mug in the sink, then Janet walked back and turned off the CD, the lights. Eventually she came into the bedroom, quietly. Rusty lay facing the wall, pretending to sleep. She heard Janet undress, a tiny tick as she undid her belt, the swish of her clothes coming off. The bed swayed as she got in. Rusty made what she thought might be a cute grunty sleeping noise. Janet patted her side and rolled to face the other way.

Rusty held Dee to herself. Janet didn't even know about her.

Janet's new art group was having Internal Conflict. Some people wanted the focus of their protest to be the new domestic workers' legislation, some people wanted it to be gay and lesbian couples, some people wanted to spend money and time contacting the mainstream media, some people wanted to spend money making slides so people could use the art in their portfolios. Kay wanted her friend Gilda to be allowed to come to meetings so she could write something for a national arts journal that Minou said she couldn't understand anyway and didn't want to talk to.

Janet thought the action at the new immigration centre was more than enough for one month. "Artists are so stupid," she said.

"Well, everyone has needs," volunteered Rusty.

"Well, are we doing a protest or writing an interminable Canada Council grant?"

Rusty didn't know. She agreed with Janet that it was stupid to turn a protest into a piece of dead art described in twenty-syllable words, but she hated that Janet did all this work that no one in the art world ever saw. If Janet really didn't want to go to university, then she should be a famous artist and she shouldn't turn down opportunities to build a career in the art world.

Rusty used to be a writer, maybe she could help Janet.

Maybe she could write some critical articles about Janet's work.

"I wish you were more concerned about your career. Maybe you could do some collaborations just with Kay, outside the group. She's the best known."

"I hate Kay. Do your own art if you want a career."

But Rusty knew she couldn't do art or even write anymore, not in her condition.

They still hadn't talked about the fight, or about the van with the cheesy mural.

Party at New Girlfriend's

Rusty has a new girlfriend. Maybe she's Dee. They've been on a couple of dates, and had sex under the pines at a provincial park and on a beach in broad daylight under a towel. But Rusty doesn't really know Dee very well.

Dee invites Rusty to a party at her house.

"I'll tell you what to wear," she says on the phone the night before.

"Christ," says Rusty to herself.

The night of the party a package containing an outfit is delivered to Rusty's house. The phone rings.

"Wear it," says Dee. She has never sounded this firm before.

"It's too small," says Rusty.

"Wear it."

It's a ridiculous outfit, so small that Rusty is hard pressed to cover herself at all. Her breasts spill out. The skirt is too short. The stockings and garter belt don't cover her nakedness, obviously, and there are no panties in the package.

She is humiliated before she walks out the door. She wears a long coat on the bus. She knows that everyone can tell that underneath she is wearing clothes that scream sex sex sex. She can feel her bare cunt against the inside of the coat when she sits down. Everyone must know. It's probably obvious: her bare cunt, waiting.

At the party Dee looks at her approvingly.

"You'll have to wait, honey. Just think about it."

Dee makes her serve drinks and snacks to the guests. Some are women Rusty has known for a long time. They know she doesn't usually dress like this. They see her acquiesce to Dee's tweaking of her exposed nipple, grabbing of her ass as she goes by. She is thoroughly embarrassed and thoroughly proud of her new girlfriend, of herself and her fuckability.

"Just you wait," says Dee in the kitchen.

Later, when the party winds down, Dee fucks her in the bedroom. Rusty comes and Dee licks her cunt until she comes again.

Rusty couldn't wake up. She tried. She got out of bed and drank juice, but all she could think about was bed.

Rusty is lying in bed. The doorbell rings, she ignores it. The door opens. She hears a half-familiar voice call her name.
"Rusty?"
"In here."
It's Dee. She is carrying a flyer about the Tai Chi place. She sits on the bed. She feels Rusty's forehead. Her fingers wander to Rusty's mouth. Rusty sucks them. Dee moves her fingers in Rusty's mouth. With her other hand she moves the covers down. Rusty grasps her collar and pulls her down next to her. They are rolling and kissing. The phone rings, one two three four. They are both naked panting kissing rocking. When Dee comes, her breath is hot and fast in Rusty's face.
"Thanks for coming over," says Rusty.
"See you around," says Dee, licking her finger.

Rusty felt great.
She thought back on her conversation at lunch with Lara and Dee. She decided that Dee had found her witty. She preferred not to think about the other time with Eagle. Anyway, Dee didn't seem to think she was a dork. Far from it. Rusty was hot.

"Thanks for coming over," whispered Rusty to herself. "See you around," she whispered, and licked her finger.

Delicious.

If Dee was going to be coming over in the afternoons, she thought, she had better get fit.

"I called, but I guess you were asleep," Janet said when she came home.

"I guess so," said Rusty. She hadn't bothered to check her messages. "I slept most of the day but I needed to, probably. I thought I'd go for a swim tonight. I need to work on my muscle tone. Do you want to come?"

"How come you're so energetic?"

"What do you mean, how come I'm so energetic? I slept the whole day, I better be energetic. Come swimming. We can go to the library on the way back. I haven't read anything good in ages."

On the way back from swimming, TV light shone blue in houses as they went past, room after room a blue pod. Rusty's bag banged gently against her calf. Janet swung the books far forward and way back. Together they tried whistling what they thought might be Dixie. Whistling Dixie.

When Rusty (Julia) was seven, her best friend Naomi joined a swim team. Two nights a week Naomi went to practice, and Julia stayed home and watched the clock. When Naomi returned from the pool she was allowed to play with Julia. She told her all about the swim team.

There were mysterious girls Naomi knew now: Dot and Lisa and Cheryl. They each had their Own Stroke. Naomi's was Back. Dot's was Fly. Lisa's was Breast. Cheryl liked Free, which wasn't really an Own Stroke but she was good at it. Once Naomi invited her swim friends for a sleepover. They were all slightly older than Julia and they talked about swimming the whole time, about their coach and the girl Susan, who they all hated, who grabbed their feet from behind while they swam.

Julia begged her mother to let her join the swim team, but they wouldn't take her until she was older.

Naomi went to meets in Lethbridge and Red Deer, in a station wagon with all the other girls. When she was nine she was going to be allowed to go to an overnight away meet. She already knew who she was going to share a room with: her relay team, Dot and Lisa and Cheryl.

Naomi cut her hair so she could swim faster. She had two different Speedos, one for practice and one in the team colours for meets.

Julia imagined herself with them in the pool, part of the new relay team that miraculously had five girls. She would be the fastest and funnest. She would hate that girl Susan too. She would go to away meets and they would put a cot in the room so she could be with her team.

When she was finally old enough, on her first day at practice, the coach asked her to swim a length. After that he put her in a lane. It was the slowest lane, she could tell, the lane for baby eight-year-olds.

Naomi was in the next lane. She said hi and that was all.

In the locker room Naomi and Dot and Lisa and Cheryl went in one shower together.

"I hate them," said a girl in the shower with Julia.

"They're snobs," said someone else.

Naomi was in the middle of a tight squealing knot of girls by the time Julia got out of the locker room. She didn't even look Julia's way.

Julia waited for her mother with the girl from the shower, Susan. It was cold out and Susan said her hair was freezing where it stuck out from her hat. She said that if you grabbed your hair when it was frozen like that, and snapped it, it could break right off. Julia's hair was too short to freeze. She focussed on the chlorine rainbows around each streetlight.

It wasn't how she thought it would be.

Rusty can't remember

anything. Not true. She can remember things. But it feels like her memory is unreliable.

There is not much in the MS self-help books on the subject. They say everyone thinks they have memory problems, even people without MS.

Rusty has moments of total fog, she has no idea what is going on.

Sometimes she suddenly sees things that are not there. At least the books tell her that her vision is supposed to be faulty. Once the world split in two horizontally. The two halves wouldn't match. This came and went for weeks. That is a symptom of MS.

The other things could just be lunacy in the finest sense. It's as though she can't process what she sees. When people who have been blind from birth are "given" sight, they have no idea what anything is, they reach out to touch objects that are miles away. Rusty sees hulking apes in clumps of trees, balls rolling in shadows, she jumps to avoid things that aren't there. She stares to make it make sense. She never tells anyone why she is startled, or about the dogs in the road.

Sometimes she reads price tags in stores, they are clear as day, but when she looks back, there is a different price. She takes to looking at everything twice.

When Rusty is tired, she cannot read. She can see words in

the corner of her vision, but when she tries to read them, they disappear.

Rusty looks at people and they say they know her and she says, yes I remember you, and she has no idea who they are. This never happened before. She used to spend her time trying not to embarrass people by knowing and remembering too much about them.

To deal with this, Rusty tells Janet long and pointless stories about every person they see. She wants to remember. She wants to prove she can.

She thinks about a woman with Alzheimer's she heard about, who reads every licence plate and comments on the numbers like they are the person's age.

Is that what she has become?

On her way up to the Drive, Rusty checked the mailbox. She and Janet got a notice from City Hall that they were cracking down on graffiti vandals and unsafe postering. What vigilance.

She received a request from a journal in Montreal to reprint an article she had written eight years before. Why reprint that? Rusty thought. Times have changed, get with it. She remembered the article, a hyper-simplistic analysis of sexual imagery. Even at the time it came across as a bit ponderous. She, Ms. Afternoon Delight, was not trapped in the eighties.

And she got a letter. Not a bill or a notice, but a personal letter. No return address. From within the city, she read the postmark. Pale green paper, thick and textured. She drew it under her nose—was that a slight scent? She didn't open it yet. She was going to savour it while sitting with a coffee. Maybe she would run into Dee. Maybe the letter was from Dee.

With the letter in her bag, she had all the time in the world. She circled wide, to the bakery (Eccles cakes), the drugstore (toothpaste) and all the way to the used furniture place (just looking) before she came back to the coffee shop.

After she sat down with her cup, she looked in her bag. No letter. She looked in her pockets. No letter. Where had she put it? No letter, no letter. Had she been carrying it in her bad hand?

The stall in the washroom told her "V and Y were here, just passing through . . ." and a date.

At home she decided to phone Dee once and for all. She wanted to know why Dee felt she could come over and fuck her and then never phone, and whether Dee had sent that letter, and what it had said because she was quite sure Dee had sent it. Her very own *billet-doux*, and she had lost it.

Next to the phone there was a conspicuous absence where Janet's phone list had been. What was the number? Rusty couldn't remember. "I am going to phone Dee at   ," she repeated to herself, waiting for the number to come. It was a blank space.

Janet phoned.

"BJ got hold of an insurance agent who has MS. We're gonna win this thing."

"Do you know where your art group phone list is?"

"Yes, it's right here. Why?"

"No reason."

"Do you need someone's number?"

"No." Yes.

"If you do, just tell me. I didn't know you used the list. I should have asked you before I took it this morning."

"No really, it's fine, I was just tidying up and I noticed it wasn't where it used to be."

"You're tidying up?"

"So what?"

"You never tidy up."

"I do so. I'm tidying up right now." Rusty picked up some pens and put them in the can on the phone table. She straightened a pile of envelopes.

"Well I guess you do. I'm bringing the list home tonight, and someone's coming over to write a leaflet with me, if that's okay."

"Fine." Is it Dee? Just ask.

"See you."

Just ask.

"Bye."

Now Rusty had to tidy up.

Loving Fantasy

Rusty is weeping. She has been hurt by something in her life—a fall, her welfare worker, someone on the street. She comes home, lies in bed, weeping.

Her lover and another woman come into the room. Together they undress her, wordlessly. They begin stroking her body.

"Beautiful beautiful," the other woman says.

All of Rusty's body is charged by their stroking.

Suddenly, Rusty is curious about every inch of her lover's body, the soft skin, the folds. She wants to touch and both women are touching her.

Their stroking becomes sharper, more focused. One of them is sucking her nipples, one of them is licking her cunt. She can hardly stand the sweetness of it, the sighs, the sharpness of the small bites. She reaches for each of them. She lies back and feels them on her, around her. She feels fingers in her, the licking, the sucking. She is enfolded.

Of course it was Dee. When Rusty got up from her nap, there they were, Dee and Janet, side by side at the computer. Rusty heard them first from the bedroom. Now she stood in the doorway. She had carefully selected her tousled outfit. She fancied herself looking a bit like a classic butch, distant and in charge.

"Hi Rusty, you remember Dee, right?"

"Of course. Working hard?"

Dee looked up at her. "We should be done in no time, I think. By the time we've covered all the artists' names, we've already used up half the leaflet." Dee and Janet laughed, old pals that they were.

Either Dee was the coolest paramour ever or Rusty had imagined their afternoon fuck. She wished her mind was more reliable. How did you ask someone how real it was for them, anyway? And whether they had sent you a letter, which you had lost. Rusty figured she would hang around and wait for a signal. Dee might refer to the Tai Chi flyer, which she had forgotten to leave behind anyway. Or maybe she would ask Rusty whether she had gotten lots of sleep the other day. Rusty could think of millions of ways that Dee could signal to her that they needed to talk.

Dee used none of them. Rusty tried to think of something

she could say to impress her and remind her how fabulous, she, Rusty, was.

"Dee was saying that she knows of a good Tai Chi place for people with MS," said Janet.

"Oh really," said Rusty, taking her cue. "Do you have, like, a flyer about it or anything?"

"I lost the piece of paper," said Dee. What did that mean? "But I can give you the number if you're interested."

"Sure," said Rusty. She didn't want to take Tai Chi. This was stupid.

"I have it at home. You should call me."

"Okay." I will, thought Rusty, and then I will go down the back lane to your house where we will discuss our nascent affair. She looked at Dee's firm back, her working hands. The fingers in her mouth. The rolling rocking kissing.

"We decided that the focus of the action is going to be the many hoops and injustices in the immigration system," Janet said. "Then we can list them all. Each artist is making a mask about their issue. And we will leave a permanent installation in the elevator. Leesa is going to play the woman who confronts the issues."

It sounded piecemeal to Rusty, though she was afraid to say so. She wanted to come across as a genius, not a spoilsport.

"What about media?"

"The local art magazine isn't interested unless we repeat the action in a gallery later. Kay wants to but I think she might be on her own. It's kind of meaningless."

"I thought I might write something for *Crash*," Rusty tried to sound blasé. "If I'm up to it, I mean."

"You write for *Crash*?" said Dee. Rusty had never had anything accepted by *Crash*, but she could still write for them. In a larger sense.

"Yeah, since when do you write for *Crash*?" said Janet.

Rusty looked mysterious and left the room.

Two Ends of Sleep

Rusty was once a cross-country champion.

She ran every morning.

Now she could never even think of doing that. It's not that MS took running away from her. She stopped long before the MS. But now she can't run at all.

Rusty is always watching her balance. Her left foot drags. When she runs, she is terrified. She feels each of the accidents she has had, landing on cement, glasses skewed. Once, her head rammed against a fence. Scraped knees. Swollen knees. "Are you all right?" Yes, no, yes, let me cry, why did you see me? I am fine, let me cry, oh it's just the MS ha-ha, I want to go home home home.

Best not to run.

At the local carnival she stands outside a fun house with Janet.

"Come on," says Janet "I know it's ridiculous, but this whole place is ridiculous." All Rusty can see are wacky shifting floors, children running light-footed through the rotating tunnel. She doesn't care, really. She just wishes she could go so she didn't have to say why she can't.

Oddly, carpets are the worst. Her sensible rubber-soled shoes stick. Once she wiped out just walking down a hall. She could hear the lesbians nearby ignoring her. She was thankful. She knew they were thinking about what a tragedy she is.

Hurrying for the bus she feels her jerky steps, fear marking each one.

Rusty saw the van again. It was driving slowly along the Drive ahead of her, looking for parking. Looking for attractive lesbians to pick up and take home, more likely. Rusty could see the mural on the side, she knew it had to be the same van. How many people in Vancouver could have wanted that mural? Perhaps the mural was the result of a hobby, like if you went to someone's house and they had framed 3-D pictures of gnomes or macramé plant hangers, then you knew they had a hobby.

Maybe the mural came in a kit.

The van turned down Rusty's street. The van was looping the block, probably. Hoping to see Janet.

It was gone by the time she rounded the corner.

The phone rings while Rusty is asleep. She pulls herself up out of a dream, answers. It's Dee.

"Hi. Rusty. Hey, it was pretty hard to stay cool the other night, with Janet right there and everything."

"Yes. I kept looking at your fingers."

"I kept looking at your lips. I kept thinking about your bed, right there in the next room."

"Me too. In the next room. I'd like to see your room. I'd like to see your fingers and you in your room very soon."

"Call me. I'm nearby. Got to go."

"Bye."

When Janet got home, Rusty woke up. They ate together. Rusty wrote a letter to the Montreal journal, telling them what she would like to add to the old article before they reprinted it. She wrote a fax to *Crash* about her proposed article on Janet's immigration action. She spent some time in the bathroom, trying to decide whether she should pierce her nipple. She fell asleep, later, her face nuzzling Janet's neck.

Janet got up and worked on her mask. Talked on the phone, typed on the computer. Rusty heard it all, half asleep on the couch. Janet back on the phone, gossiping.

"Yeah, Dee thinks she's really something. 'Babe' is the word she used, if you can believe it."

Who? Who did Dee think was a "babe"? Her? Babe. Why would she tell Janet?

Rusty hated women who called other women "babe." Dee was better when she didn't talk. But here was the Catch-22: either Rusty was Dee's babe, blecch, or some other woman was. Eagle? Who was Dee "babe"-ing, if not Rusty? Answer that, Dee-Dee, Tai Chi.

She had to phone her.

"Where did you go that night?" Rusty asked Janet. She didn't have to say what night. They both knew what night. Rusty thought of it as the Van Night.

"Out."

They were lying in bed, naked. Janet had her back to Rusty. Rusty was letting her hand snake from between Janet's legs, up the crack of Janet's ass and back again.

"Come on, Janet."

"Okay, okay. I went to the bar."

"The bar?" Janet hardly ever went to the bar. They hardly ever went to the bar.

"Yes, the bar. I had a good time. I might go again sometime." Janet was leaning back slightly. Rusty slid her hand between her breasts.

"What was so great about it anyway?" asked Rusty.

"Are you jealous? You can storm out next time if you want," said Janet.

"I just want to know what was so fucking great." She kissed Janet's shoulder.

"I didn't say it was great."

"Who was there that I know?" Rusty wanted to know if someone else knew about their fight. She didn't want anyone to know.

"Nobody. I'll tell you what, though. I met someone you might like. I think she's kind of into time travel." That mural.

"I'm not into time travel. Don't make fun of me." But Rusty was laughing.

"Tell me that fantasy. I won't laugh. I'll let you be in charge."

Janet rolled back and lay still on the bed. Rusty told her a story. A story that had Janet pleading, arching her pelvis, raising her mouth closer closer.

"All I could think about was you," said Janet. When? It didn't matter.

"You know," said Janet, "that fantasy doesn't really put you in charge."

"In charge enough," said Rusty.

"Yes."

Then Rusty let Janet bite her, leave purple marks all over her, run red welts down her back, slide up and down Rusty's leg till she came. She asked for everything. Nothing mattered.

The Experiment

Rusty has agreed to help out in an experiment. All weekend she's been making eyes at this woman scientist, and the scientist is responding, clearly *and* cautiously. At dinner she pulled a classic, spilling her wine on Rusty's shirt, wiping in circles at Rusty's nipple while her other hand rested on Rusty's knee.

It is all rather suspect. The lab is in a country house, the scientist is dressed in a weird outfit—a long tight vest over a baggy white shirt, and pants that tie at the knee.

"Please take off your clothes," says the scientist. "The machine is not strong enough for clothes."

"What machine?"

The scientist ignores her. "Please, the clothes," she repeats.

"Okay, okay."

Rusty is naked. She shivers. It is damp in the country house. She wishes the scientist would just get on with it—it being sex—since why else would she want Rusty naked?

The scientist is aloof and excited. Her authority is seductive. Rusty's nipples are erect in the cold.

"Stand here," says the scientist, and places Rusty in a circle marked on the damp floor. "Stand still," she mocks, slapping Rusty's ass. It smarts.

There is a flash.

Rusty finds herself alone in a ditch by a road. She is naked, it is daytime in the country. She doesn't know where she is.

Men walk down the road. Rusty crouches in the grass. They are dressed like the scientist and speaking in a language she almost understands. She stays low. No one sees her.

Rusty ponders her situation. She has no clothes and doesn't speak the language. She has no idea where she is. The grass pricks her naked body. When she feels her breasts her nipples are still hard. Her ass still smarts. Her cunt aches longingly.

She is still ready to fuck.

Serves her right for lusting after such a weirdo.

Then she is saved. The scientist is here, driving a rickety cart pulled by a slow, tired horse.

"Welcome to Medieval England!" she exclaims. Suddenly the clothes make sense. Suddenly Rusty feels very naked. Suddenly she knows what she wants.

The scientist lifts her up to the cart's seat. "You are shivering," she says to Rusty and wraps her in a blanket.

Rusty lets the scientist put an arm around her.

They ride past the group of men, who greet the scientist enthusiastically. The scientist is confident and capable—she knows the language, she knows the men. Her eyes are gleaming as she looks at Rusty in anticipation. Rusty wraps the blanket closer, feels the wool tease her skin.

Finally they are alone on the road. The scientist reaches one hand under the blanket. Rusty feels her body respond. She feels the rush of this strange situation, the scientist's callused palm. For the first time all weekend she really notices the scientist's lips, cupid-shaped, wet and eager.

"Do you like this experiment so far?" says the scientist.

"Yes," says Rusty in a low voice, reaching to pull the scientist closer. Their kiss is long and deep. The scientist's chest is rising and falling, her breath is short. As Rusty pulls the scientist on top of her she can feel their heartbeats, the scientist's under her hand, her own ringing in her ear.

They roll off the seat of the cart, into the hay stacked behind. Rusty drops the blanket on the hay, whispering "You want me" as the scientist reaches to touch her.

"I do," says the scientist. "So help me."

The scientist's cunt is slippery and warm. She moans when Rusty slides her finger down.

"Yes," she says.

"Yes," says Rusty. "Oh yes. Tell me you like it."

Her fingers find their own path, deeper, deeper. The scientist is tossing her head from side to side, she scratches Rusty's back. Her shirt is pulled up and her breasts spring round from her chest. Rusty sucks each one. She rubs her own cunt on the scientist's thigh and taunts her with her nipples. The bow-shaped lips reach again and again. The sun is hot.

"I like Medieval England," mutters Rusty lazily into the scientist's shoulder.

"I'll teach you what you need to know," says the scientist. "You just need to know how to say 'fuck me.' "

They both laugh.

"Here is another sentence for you," says the scientist. "It means 'I am a slut.' " Rusty repeats it.

"I'm going now," adds the scientist, sitting up. And is gone.

There is no second flash. Rusty remains.

The men are coming down the road to the cart.

Rusty pulls her blanket close.

"Fuck me," she says feebly. "I am a slut."

Rusty watched the kids in the barren yard across the street. One of them, the girl, held a board like a chainsaw.

"Rrrrrmmmmm," she said. "Rrrrrmmmmm. Rrrrrmmmmm." She had straight, dark brown hair in a ponytail and large brown eyes that squinted while she sawed. She was wearing a blue sweatshirt that said "Bones." Rusty couldn't figure out the shirt, but then again, what did she know about the world of nine-year-olds? It could mean anything.

The girl went to each spot in the yard where a tree had been. "Rrrrrmmmmm." She looked like she was having a pretty good time.

There were lots of other kids in the yard. They were all ignoring the chainsawer. They were playing something that involved a lot of rules. They would run around for a few minutes, someone would call a halt and they would all gather in a mess of bright children's clothing colours and argue. Then they would all run around again. The chainsaw massacrer was definitely getting more sustained amusement. Neither the man nor the woman was in sight.

Rusty received a fax from *Crash* about her proposal. She had to go to the local stationery store to pick it up.

The fax didn't say much. Their submission guidelines. *Crash* had quirky letterhead with the gonzo flavour of the magazine. The guidelines were less interesting. She had to send them samples of her writing and a detailed outline of the article she proposed. They would take her on spec and they could refuse to publish her piece without paying her anything.

Rusty had hoped they would be more eager to have her. Janet was impressed anyway.

"Wow," she said. "It's like living with Dorothy Parker."

"Thanks," snarled Rusty, though she was pleased.

After reading the guidelines, Rusty spent some time making faces in the mirror, looking the way *Crash* writers looked in their contributors' photos She saw herself in a coffee shop, smoking, discussing sex and nihilism. Better yet, in a New York diner, a loner who cool young people recognized by sight. An Andy Warhol type. "Ha-ha-ha," she laughed with her friends as she walked with her distinctive gait down the crowded pavements of Manhattan.

She would be in Manhattan because once she became a regular and favoured writer with *Crash*, she would move to New York to write her trendy irreverent column for the *Village*

Voice. Rusty would live every New York fantasy she had ever had. Sarah Schulman's greatest ally in the Lesbian Avengers. Discovered as a great actor. Leading member of the Guerilla Girls. Living in the Dakota. Living in a squat. Friend of major rock stars. An underground rock star herself. Friend of down-and-out jazz musicians. It was a long list.

Back in Vancouver, Dee would read about Rusty and impulsively book flights so they could have torrid trysts.

At the Chelsea Hotel.

Rusty is lying in bed with all her clothes on. Her pants are undone—for circulation while she sleeps. Her hand is nestled inside the zipper. She hears the door. Squeak.

Rusty keeps her eyes closed, listening. The squeak is followed by padding footsteps. Someone coughs. A woman. Janet? Or a woman who is not a very good burglar. First squeaking, then coughing. And now putting on music! It must be Janet. Rusty hears the clicking of a case and the player, then slow moaning blues singing, guitar and South Asian string music. Rusty doesn't recognize it. Janet must have bought a new CD.

The door opens. It's not Janet. It's Dee.

"Do you like this?" she asks.

You coming over like this?

"What? The music?"

"Yeah. I just bought it. Don't you think it's kind of luxurious? I mean it's so slow," says Dee.

"It's beautiful," says Rusty. And it is. Unhurried, sinuous, clear and precise. A man is singing in English. Blues. Really slow. It is impossibly beautiful.

"I like music when I'm making love," says Dee, sitting on the bed by Rusty.

"Me too," says Rusty.

Dee pulls Rusty's hand from her pants and slides her own hand in. Dee's hand is cool against Rusty's vulva. Dee's finger slides easily. Rusty must be wet.

"You're wet," says Dee. "Why's that?"

"You," says Rusty. She can't concentrate. The finger is moving up and down. Dee's other hand is moving in her shirt. Dee is pulling on her nipple.

The music is low and constant. It is still the same tune. Every possible nuance of the song is slowly unravelling, stretching. Rusty is being unravelled too, stretched between the poles of her nipple and her cunt.

When Dee's fingers finally reach inside, Rusty rubs her own clitoris until she comes. She feels dizzy, like her brain has been replaced with candy floss.

"You're beautiful," says Dee, pulling her fingers out slowly. She raises her hand to her mouth and slowly licks her finger.

Rusty smiles.

"I'll see you soon," says Dee, getting up.

She turns the music down and takes the CD out, click click. Squeak, she leaves the house.

Rusty woke up.

It was the CD again, the low resonant voice, the patient wailing strings. This time with a hint of gospel.

Outside the window, the sun had gone down and the sky was shifting colours, a high dark blue to a low robin's egg. Someone was cooking something in the kitchen. Dee?

Rusty struggled awake and out of the bedroom.

"Hi honey!" said Janet.

Janet.

"I got the CD—*Mumtaz Mahal*. Remember, we heard it at Lara's that time? I love it."

Right. Now Rusty remembered.

"Yeah, it's great. So slow and luxurious," she said. She kissed Janet. "It is beautiful," she said.

"I'm glad you like it," said Janet.

Her future *Crash*–writer-self burning strong, Rusty went to Red Letters, a radical bookstore with lots of old magazines. She needed to check out back issues of *Crash*.

When she walked in was the best part, when *Crash*-writer Rusty could impress whoever was hanging in the reading room. She hadn't been to Red Letters in a while. There were changes —Nicaragua had been cut back to one shelf—but her old friend Kyle was still behind the cash. Did Kyle really think anyone still cared about the Spanish Civil War?

"Rusty!" he said. "I haven't seen you in a long time."

"I haven't been around much," said Rusty. "Do you have any back issues of *Crash*, Kyle?"

"You mean *Trash*? We don't carry that shit, Rusty. You know that. It's just a waste of paper."

Some women on the couch looked up from their anarchist zines. They probably read *Crash*, in secret. Rusty knew she could still turn heads.

"Oh. Well, I'm about to write something for them. I wanted to check out the competition."

"Why are you writing for *them*?" asked one of the couch women.

None of your business. Ever hear of readership? thought Rusty

" 'Cause they'll pay me," she said instead.

She went to the library for the back issues. *Crash* published articles by famous writers about funny events in their lives, and quirky photos of young skinny people at supposedly important events, and pieces about up-and-coming artists and filmmakers. She took notes like she was supposed to, on point of view and the ratio of facts to personal opinion.

Rusty sat in bed. She stared out the window and watched the house across the street. Now that she could see it. Like a cowardly private eye, too chicken to leave her own house. A woman Rusty once met had gone to private eye school. She described creepy tests like entering, searching and exiting the residence of a stranger when they weren't home, without leaving a trace. Rusty thought of herself as more like Jimmy Stewart in *Rear Window*, just observing. From where Rusty sat she could see anything that happened in the yard, and some things that happened inside the house.

On nice days, the woman who lived there sat on her front steps and watched the kids. She wore jeans and smoked cigarettes. One day, a friend stopped by and sat with her. A few times, Rusty saw the woman head up to the Drive with the children in tow. The small boy bounced up and down like a metal spring. When she came back, Rusty could see her walk slowly through the living room on her way to the kitchen. Once, in her yard, the woman laughed for a long time.

The man was lying low.

The next time Rusty saw the van, it was already parked. Rusty had come out to sit on the porch and wait for Janet to get home from work, and there it was. On her street.

On her street.

What was the scoop? Had the van moved here? She had never seen it before that night and now it was here all the time. Circling the block. Parking. She felt watched.

Why should she have to sit here and stare at that van? It just reminded her.

Then, like a Magic Eye puzzle, Rusty stared long enough and an image was revealed. A woman in a softball uniform walked down the sidewalk and around to the driver's side of the van. Vanwoman. Rusty's competition, the time traveller. As she fumbled for her keys Rusty got a good look.

She was young. Younger than Rusty, and pierced. Pfeh, thought Rusty. Piercing. So what. Vanwoman had a ring in her eyebrow and another in her nose. She was wearing a baseball cap, with no hair showing. She had full lips and a tight body.

Vanwoman plunged Rusty into despair with her youth and perkiness and softball playing. Things Rusty could never offer Janet. Rusty imagined Janet at Vanwoman's games, cheering her on. Finally Janet would be able to hang out with women her own age. No wonder. Rusty saw the appeal herself. Unless of course Vanwoman only pretended to play softball, just to meet dykes, to have affairs with unsuspecting women like Janet. Rusty imagined her wearing the uniform, seducing Janet in the bar, taking her to the street to make out in her van.

Poor Janet.

The van left and Rusty went inside to wait for Janet. She wouldn't tell her what she knew.

At the grocery store

Rusty always gets a cart. Even if she has to go to a cashier to get change because the cart costs a quarter. Even if all she is buying is a carton of milk. The cart is a walker, a young person's version of the wheeled cages that old people use.

Rusty doesn't mind appearing lazy.

Well, she does mind, but for some reason she would rather appear lazy than disabled.

On the bus Rusty doesn't give up her seat anymore. She even scrambles with other people to sit down when she can. "No, you take it," they say insincerely, eyeing her young and trim body. They don't really mean it, but she takes the seat.

I can't stand up that long. I can't stand on a bus. I'll fall over, she says to herself. I've got a disability, goddammit, I deserve this.

But she never says this out loud. She has never said to anyone standing next to her while she sits in the sweaty bus, "Sorry, I have MS and I have to sit down." My oh my, even without saying it she knows the distance that would open. It might be a sympathetic distance, so fucking what? It's still there.

There is a line. On one side are the happy people in scooters and bus seats near the front, and on the other are the lazy people with carts. Rusty clings to her side. She will cling for as long as she can.

Intending to write for *Crash* and actually writing for *Crash* were two different things. Even writing the proposal was a stretch. Rusty thought of Chairman Mao. The longest march begins with a single step. Only it wasn't exactly like that because she hadn't meant to take the single step, yet here she was, on the road. Now she had to take the next step because everyone was watching.

"I thought you hated *Crash*," said Janet.

Rusty was trying to write an outline for *Crash* and all anyone could do was bring up old shit.

"Well, I do hate *Crash* but I still want to write for them."

"You told me you would never write for them because their articles have no content and 'all they're interested in doing is using supposedly witty writing to trash people on the margins.' That's practically a direct quote," said Janet proudly.

"Yeah, well, I changed my mind. If I want to be a writer, I have to write for magazines that pay me. I want to have a career."

"Writing for *Crash*?"

"It's not that stupid. Lots of people like it."

"I know. That's what you used to think was so sick about it, remember? 'Why are people seduced by this garbage?' "

"You should be glad. It's your art action I'm writing about."

"Correction, my group's art action. I'm not even sure I like it anymore. And anyway, *Crash* is definitely not going to let you write about the issues and you know it. I don't know why everyone's so excited about this."

"Who's excited?"

"People in my group."

"About my article?"

Rusty couldn't ask if Dee was excited, but it had to be Dee who told the group about *Crash*. Janet would never bother. Janet had this idea that it wasn't the artist's job to find people to write about their art. She was very pure.

The next day, Rusty spent a long time choosing the right outfit to phone Dee so she would be ready when Dee asked her over. She wanted just the right balance between hip and mature. It had to have an element of sexiness, but not be over the top. She wanted to be irresistible, but still have dignity if Dee turned her down. Casual, yet chic. Colourful, yet muted. And above all it had to look like she had just thrown it on.

"What, this old thing?" she pictured herself saying. She practised in front of the mirror. "What, this old thing?"

She was still too skinny and flabby. More swimming.

When she finally phoned Dee, the phone rang and rang and then the machine came on. Who else lived there?

Rusty left a message about Tai Chi.

Janet came home and suggested they go out. For once. The bar. Rusty, of course, was already perfectly dressed. Janet was amazed that Rusty didn't want to spend her usual hours getting ready to go out. Rusty acted like she just happened to have thrown on the perfect outfit for any occasion.

"I've changed," said Rusty. "I can just go in what I'm wearing. I don't care. This old thing?"

At the bar, they sat in the back corner. Rusty watched the dancing and the pool and the cruising. A woman came over to the table and talked to Janet for a bit, then looked embarrassed and left. Rusty kept an eye out for Vanwoman.

Janet was vibrating next to her. They had this connection, and in the past Rusty could swear that their cunts communicated. It defied science. She hadn't felt it recently but she felt it now. She put her hand on Janet's shoulder.

Janet reached under the table and undid Rusty's jeans. Rusty let out a moan of surprise and excitement and sat poised on Janet's fingers, rocking gently to feel them hard against her clit.

"Let's dance," said Janet. She took her hand away and stood up. Rusty followed, her cunt leading.

Janet was a beautiful dancer. She always looked as though dancing was the last thing on her mind. Rusty was nervous about her balance, felt her feet rooted. At a slow number, Rusty went to sit down, Janet wouldn't let her, held her in a dark corner of the floor. Slid her hand in her shirt, rubbed slow against her leg.

Back at the table, Rusty was dizzy. Under the table, Janet's hand was insistent on her cunt; above, her tongue in her mouth, her fingers in her mouth. Dee, thought Rusty briefly. The music was blaring. Women were playing pool only yards away. She was lost in her own mouth, her own cunt, her own body.

"Fuck me," she whispered.

"Here?" said Janet.

"Yes, here. Yes, please." And the fingers, one, two, three, her head exploded, she would have sworn it.

"You owe me one," said Janet.

In a bathroom stall at the bar, Rusty read "Dykes Rule," "I love pussy," and lots of names.

On the street it was late and empty. Cars sat one by one, expectant, at the curb.

Rusty had read freelance writers' manuals. She knew what the *Crash* sketch should be. It had to say what kind of article she had in mind, which sources she would use and how fabulously original it would be. She also had to include published samples of her recent writing.

This last was a bit of a problem. Rusty's best published writing had appeared in teeny-weeny leftist and feminist newspapers, and even when her articles were appropriate to *Crash* (which they mostly weren't), they were always next to something that really wasn't. Plus they were all at least two years old.

Janet was no help.

"Just tell them you've been sick lately and that's why you haven't written anything," she suggested.

"Yeah right. Like they want someone who never leaves the house."

"Well you don't really leave the house, so maybe you are the wrong person for this."

"Look, it's fine, okay? Just help me clip away the other articles so they don't know what the publication is like."

"You're going to try to pretend that *Proletarian Voice* is targeted at yuppies?"

Janet thought if *Crash* didn't like Rusty's politics, Rusty shouldn't write for them. Rusty was willing to lie.

Maybe they weren't really arguing about *Crash*. Maybe they were really fighting about Dee and Vanwoman, neither of whom ever came up in conversation.

Dee, Rusty thought, would have been more of a help than Janet. At least her attitude was right. But Rusty couldn't admit to her that things were even the slightest bit iffy with *Crash*. She soldiered on and wrote a vague sketch.

She told *Crash* she would outline the local (that is, Canadian) political situation and the artists involved, interview artists and audience, and include her own "wry" commentary. She would set the whole thing in a larger context so readers would understand the significance of contemporary street art. "As a tool for social change," she added and then deleted. She took out the bit about the significance of street art and said she would bear in mind that she was writing for a national audience. She took out the political part, then put it back in because how could you write about political art without the politics?

"*Crash* does it all the time," said a little voice that sounded remarkably like Janet's.

Her *Crash* fantasies were sponge dinosaurs that grew in the sink until they were puffy and soft and bright. The reality of writing for *Crash* sucked away the water and the fantasies shrank back to the little desiccated worms they really were.

Or they were a family of beautiful cockroaches with shells like enamelled jewellery, scuttling freely in the darkness of the kitchen and then running back to the safety of the stove whenever a light came on.

How had Rusty gotten herself into this? How had Rusty become the one who pulled the plug, switched on the light, crushed the colours in her own head?

Rusty gets magazines

from the MS society. She likes them. They are full of information and questions that doctors never bring up. Like, if you have just started dating someone, how soon do you tell them you have MS? This is familiar to Rusty. If you have just met someone, how soon do you tell them you are a lesbian? Her friend Lara says, how soon do you tell them you have been in the psych ward? (Maybe never.) How soon do you tell them you can't read? (Probably never.) How soon do you tell them you did time? And so on. The world is apparently full of people wondering how soon they should reveal their most nagging secret.

Once Rusty sees an ad for a scooter called the Scamper. In the ad, a woman in a floral print shirt—correction, blouse—and *slacks* (Rusty is sure they are slacks) is sitting on her Scamper in a suburban kitchen. She is taking cookies out of the oven, offering them to two smiling children. What a scamp! Rusty and Janet laugh uproariously about the Scamper ads.

Sean downstairs has AIDS, which is very different from having MS. First, for all the obvious reasons—like, MS is usually not fatal. Also, Rusty is quite sure that no one is trying to market scampiness to PWAS. When Sean had to tell his parents he had AIDS, it was as big a deal as coming out. When Sean had to find a place to live, keep his job, go swimming, AIDS AIDS AIDS. When Sean goes on a date, he knows when the right time is to tell them he has AIDS. Sean is pretty cheerful, considering.

Sean wants to stay alive now, as much as Rusty wants to sleep.

Rusty reads about who gets MS. People like her, it turns out. More women than men and more white people than any other racial group. No one knows why. Dairy products are the culprit, say some sources.

To read the books, you'd think it was also a disease of only straights, that strikes only members of nuclear families, only people who have real jobs.

You can tell anyone you have MS. It's not embarrassing. They won't think you're a pervert. You can read about yourself on bus posters. Three women with MS were on Gzowski, on national radio. Rusty's mother phoned her.

The phone rings. Rusty answers as best she can from her nap.

"Hi."

"Hello?" says Rusty.

"It's me." It's Dee.

"Hi," says Rusty.

"Are you alone?" asks Dee.

"Yes," says Rusty. "Do you want to come over?" Her pulse is quickening. She is ready.

"No, I want to talk to you."

"Why?"

"I like talking on the phone. I like knowing you're listening."

"Oh."

"What are you wearing?" asks Dee.

"Shirt, pants."

"Does the shirt have buttons?"

"Yeah."

"Undo them."

"It's hard with the phone—"

"Are you undoing them?"

"Yes."

"Undo them all."

"Okay, I have."

"What's underneath?"

"My breasts."

"Touch them."

Rusty holds the phone in one hand and cups her breast with the other. Smooth and cool. Dee's voice is in her ear. Dee never stops.

"Are you touching them? Does that feel good? Tell me what it feels like. Describe it to me." Rusty can only talk in short breathy bursts. Hard hot open need. Words feel far away. Sentences are out of reach.

Dee is relentless. "I'm touching my own cunt. It's really wet, and it's aching for you. I am putting my fingers in right now." Dee moans. "Oh that feels good. Are you hot now, do you wish I was there?"

"Yes, I wish you were here," Rusty manages. "I want you."

"You're not touching your cunt yet are you?"

"No," gasps Rusty. She is lying. "No. I haven't. Can I?"

"Not yet. Remember I can always come over. And if you've been touching yourself—"

Please, come over, thinks Rusty.

"Okay, undo your pants."

Finally. It goes on forever, Rusty waiting and stroking herself when she's told to, Dee talking. The orgasms are loud and sudden when they happen.

"That was nice," says Dee. "I do like knowing you listen to me."

"Yeah," says Rusty.

"You taste great," says Dee. "See ya Rusty. Bye."

Rusty has a dream. In the dream, Dee and Eagle are fucking in front of her. Rusty is jealous. She wants to join in but she doesn't know what to say. She can tell that they are performing for her. She watches Dee do all the things with Eagle that Rusty thought were hers—fingers in the mouth, rolling rocking kissing. Both of them keep looking at her, to make sure she's watching. She's too shy to join in. They laugh at her. She leaves, humiliated. Dee follows. Moving slyly with her from place to place, flirting.

Two Ends of Sleep

Rusty pointed out the treeless house to Janet.

"Look," she said, "notice anything different?"

Janet had already noticed the clearcut. She wished the trees were still there.

"Look, now the kids are coming outside," said Rusty. "They're both wearing sweatshirts today."

Janet glanced out. She didn't seem very curious.

"The man who lives there cut down the trees," said Rusty. She was staring out the window. The kids were distracted by something on the ground in the yard. Their heads were bent together, watching.

"I don't think a man lives there," said Janet.

"Well, anyway the woman seems really interesting."

The woman was sitting on the steps again, even though it was chilly. The woman who visited with her sometimes was on the sidewalk, a stocky woman with short hair, carrying a plastic bag. The friend put the bag down to talk over the fence. She used both hands when she talked.

"Hey, that's Marianne!" said Janet when she saw her. "Hey, Marianne!" she yelled out the window.

"Hey! Janet! Hi!" called the visitor.

Janet had taken away Rusty's house. Janet knew these people. She knew everyone.

"I don't really know her," said Janet reassuringly as she shut the window. "Marianne used to hang out with Felice, that poet, remember? They were both at that Aboriginal Poetry Night we went to."

The woman and Marianne had gone inside, and Rusty stared at them in the living room. They were smoking, like the women in Rusty's fantasies, like Rusty used to. Rusty knew how it would be if she ever met them. She would go over and stand in front of them like an idiot. The women would offer a cigarette and Rusty would say no. Then they would offer coffee or tea and Rusty would say she didn't drink caffeine. It was no use.

The *Crash* proposal weighed dead in Rusty's hand as she walked to the stationery store. She wanted to change it again. She wanted to reread it again. She wanted to write a note that said: "Whatever you want, I'll do it, just say." She wanted to act like it was no big deal, like she didn't give a fuck whether *Crash* wanted her or not.

She wanted to go back to bed. Her legs felt funny. She didn't usually walk this far. She wanted her old life back, before she was writing this thing.

She faxed it anyway. The longest march has many steps, each of them a beginning.

On the way back, she surveyed the curbless sidewalks of her block, the gentle slope of grass and gravel beneath the parked cars. One block down, where the gentrification started, there were curbs. It had to do with property taxes.

She walked right past her house. Her legs still felt funny. She walked right to the end of the block, to where the curbed block began, then turned so she could stay on her own poor, skinflint-taxpayer block. She walked along the bottom of her block and up the next street, right up to the Drive again. To the used bookstore on the corner.

In the window was a calculated tip of the hat to all the seventeen-year-old hippies and beatniks now living on the Drive.

Every piece of retro trippery the bookseller could find. It was a weird assortment, books that only went together in hindsight: *On the Road, Steal This Book, Soul on Ice, SCUM Manifesto*. A wave had gone out and come back in, and Rusty hadn't even noticed. She didn't even know what lay underneath, stirred up by the tide on the ocean floor. She had missed it. She had been asleep.

Inside the store was Lara.

"Check this out," she said, waving a paperback entitled *Be Here Now, Remember*. " 'Be here now.' Don't even *think* about being over there then, my friend. Baba Ram Dass. Or should I say Doctor Richard Alpert?"

Rusty looked at the book. Richard Alpert, a.k.a. Baba Ram Dass, looked very intense and soft at the same time.

"You should buy this for your spiritual development," said Lara.

"Do you ever wish you *had* been there then?" asked Rusty.

"Dropping acid, digging Janis Joplin, throwing Molotov cocktails at cops? Yeah. Fucking any guy who asked? No."

There is no halcyon past and the present is tainted by envy. Which is worse? That there is no scene anymore, or that it's under your nose and you're missing it? That you will always miss it because you are so determined not to get sucked in?

"Do you ever read *Crash*?" she asked Lara.

"I am here now," said Lara. "I don't read. It pollutes my mind."

They both laughed, standing in the bookstore.

Rusty had read too much. She had also been to too many groups, retreats, late night confessionals. She had been eager to make sense of her life. She wanted it to be a movie, with an essential conflict. She wanted to look back as a biographer and say—this led to this and this led to this and all her life she . . .

Rusty would look back and hold an object or a place in her mind until the memory came out. It was like she found an opening and pressed—and the memories flowered. They sat vividly in her, complete, blocks of experience that she rearranged over and over. Look at this—I was a tomboy. Look at this—I was a femme from day one. We were poorer than our friends. We were richer. We ate healthy in my family. We ate junk. And in every chain of pictures, she ignored whatever was grey and contradictory and emerged with something clear, as though she had just seen the truth, as though the scales had fallen from her eyes.

She talked about her past in definitives.

Sometimes she lay in bed pondering the missing piece that might pull all her troubles together. Not a piece. More like one day she would discover the end of the cord that, when she pulled it, would reveal itself snug in a tunnel of cloth, gathering everything up. Or a cord like oyster fishers use, that she could lift from the water and find her life gripped in incongruous clusters. The cord would weave a thread of imagery through all the moments she had thought were turning points, that had ended up just being things she remembered. It would gather her life into a shimmering string of moments that followed inexorably one from the other, instead of the way they felt, unattached.

Rusty tried things on for size, dipped and lifted them in her life, over and over. Faith was not her problem. Or maybe it was. Rusty wanted faith, no matter what kind. She wished for the capacity to follow blindly. She wanted her head to stop. She wanted to be gullible, to follow her heart and not care what people thought.

Now Rusty lay in bed with books about personal change. Read the testimonies and the lives defined by chiselled troubles, saw the glistening eyes of converts on the book jackets. She let them in, but woke up the next day wondering: Why are they making so much money? or: What about rape?

If only she could believe. If only she could stop wanting so badly to believe.

Outside Laundr-Eeze was the van, mural and all.

Vanwoman must have had a crisis, felt a need to launder some woman's underthings that had been flung across the van in a moment of passion. Or maybe her own gritty Perfect True Lesbian softball uniform. Maybe she picked women up in Laundr-Eeze and then boffed them in the van while the dryer turned relentlessly. Then they folded together on the chipped folding table, discreetly avoiding each other's underwear, cracking laundry jokes about mismatched socks.

Little did those women know that the underthings they set aside were not even Vanwoman's, that the softball uniform was just a ploy. If they came back tomorrow they could go out to the lane and see Vanwoman grinding her uniform into the grass and gravel for realistic stains. They would see their own mislaid underclothes tastefully eschewed by the new woman, the next in the chain.

Rusty stood in front of the laundromat. She looked in the window. Vanwoman was talking to the woman who gave out change and did your laundry too, if you paid extra. Vanwoman seemed in a rush and she seemed a bit upset. Rusty had an impulse to know what was going on. She propped the door open.

"You said my stuff would be ready at noon, and it's already quarter after four and it's still in the dryer." Vanwoman was practically yelling. "I've got a game to get to."

"Sorry. Five minutes," said the Laundr-Eeze woman. "You come back."

"No, I need this stuff right away. I'm staying."

Vanwoman was muttering now, something that sounded like, "And then I'm never coming back."

Wow.

She seemed a bit harsh but nonetheless very impressive. Rusty only dreamed about saying things like that to unhelpful people in stores. Vanwoman exuded anger even as she sat. She hadn't brought a book like everyone else. She just hunched with her back to the door, apparently glaring at the dryer in front of her.

Rusty turned back to the van. Site of Janet's betrayal, the lure that flickered silver in the deep when Janet closed her eyes. She moved onto the street so she could look in the driver-side window without Vanwoman seeing her. The seat had a fuzzy blue cover. A plastic St. Christopher hung from the rearview mirror. The space between the front seats was filled with junk—paper, pens, tapes, an empty beer can. Rusty looked up. On the ceiling was a poster of a medieval warrior—a woman named Elzru with very large breasts.

The tape deck was Alpine. Expensive. Rusty could see the speaker in the passenger door. The deck itself could be removed when you left the van, but Vanwoman hadn't bothered. On the floor of the passenger side was a red lock that went on the steering wheel. Vanwoman hadn't bothered with that either. She was just picking up her laundry, Rusty had heard her say. She was in a rush. There was a baseball glove and cap on the passenger seat.

What was it like being Vanwoman, picking up women to have a quickie under Elzru's watchful gaze, tossing the ball around on hot days, choosing an airbrush scene to go next to your heartshaped window? How did Vanwoman feel as she sat high above the road on her fuzzy blue seat? What was in the back of that van anyway?

The door was open. Sometimes our spirit guides have adventures in store for us.

Rusty looked at Laundr-Eeze. Five minutes must be up, but Vanwoman was stuck in the chair. There are things in life you want wet. Laundry is not one of them.

Rusty climbed into the van.

She *was* Vanwoman. She sat in the driver's seat, she rolled down the window and propped her arm on the door as she had seen Vanwoman do that day on her street. She rummaged through the tapes as though to choose one and pop it in the Alpine. All Melissa Etheridge. She turned around and looked in the back. It was camperized, maybe mobile-homerized. There was a bed/sofa, a small sink, more empty beer cans, another poster. Brindlorava. What a pair of hooters. You had to notice.

She turned back and feigned driving. Rusty had never imagined the van as an automatic. Vanwoman seemed to think she was Tough City, she should at least drive a standard and smoke Player's. But if she was going to fuck women in the street outside the bar, it had to be a van and an automatic.

The only butt in the ashtray was a More. There was no excuse for that.

Rusty picked up the baseball mitt on the passenger seat and

tried it on. It fit her left hand, which made her think that Vanwoman was left-handed. She had never worn a baseball mitt in her life. This was a true lesbian moment. She slapped her right fist into the palm of the glove.

"Batter up," she muttered. "Let's play ball."

There were keys underneath the mitt. On a key chain with a little baseball. Okay, maybe a softball. Rusty didn't know the difference.

Keys.

She glanced over at Laundr-Eeze. The dryer was still tumbling, Vanwoman's shoulders still exuded impatience.

One key had a black plastic top. It fit the ignition.

Vroom-vroom, Rusty thought. She turned the key to Accessory and put on Melissa Etheridge, real low. She took the More out of the ashtray and pretended to smoke.

A car pulled up next to her. The passenger rolled down the window.

"Are you on your way? We'd like the space."

Rusty should have said, "No, I'm just waiting here," Or, if she had been thinking faster, "No, I'm just parking." She should have gotten out of the van.

But Rusty had an instant, reflexive, purely Canadian response to any implication that she was in the way.

"Oh sorry," she said, "I'm just going."

And she started the van and pulled out. It was that easy. The van was big, but it had power steering. In the rearview mirror, she expected to see Vanwoman bolting out of Laundr-Eeze, but what with the noise of the dryers and her back to the door, she must not have noticed. Instead, Rusty saw the car move into her space. Laundr-Eeze got smaller and smaller.

What to do next? She knew that what she *should* do was take the van back to Laundr-Eeze, park it somewhere, get out and walk away. Leave the keys on the seat. Walk away.

But Rusty had not anticipated the adrenalin rush of this kind of law-breaking. It was better than shoplifting, better than standing in front of a monster truck that was going to log the rainforest while your friends sang "We Shall Overcome" by the side of the road. Or at least as good. She felt really wild, like the girls in high school who dropped acid at lunch and went on the roof of the gym and threw things on cop cars. The ones she wanted to be friends with, but she was too nerdy. Now she was a felon, driving around in a stolen vehicle. She felt like Thelma and Louise, or Peter Fonda in *Easy Rider*, or the killers in *Badlands*. She cranked the volume on the Alpine.

Too bad it was Melissa Etheridge.

Rusty was heading to Big J's Flowers. The van was almost facing that direction to begin with, towards the West End. She passed a women's baseball game. Was this where Vanwoman was supposed to be? she wondered. She might have recognized the uniform from the stripe in the dryer, from the cap on the seat, but she couldn't risk slowing down in case Vanwoman's teammates spotted the van.

On Davie Street she did slow down outside the flower store, hoping Janet would look up and catch a glimpse of her driving by. Then she might learn something about how they arranged their trysts, like maybe Janet had a signal she gave the van.

Nothing. The store was impassive, a wall of reflective glass. Cars behind Rusty honked impatiently when she slowed to a crawl. She decided to drive around the block and try again. On the second pass, a man came out of the store with a box of what could only be long-stemmed roses. Rusty had never really thought about how capital R Romantic Janet's job was. Still, the face of the window wasn't giving anything away.

On the third pass, Rusty gave a little honk. The van had a loud horn, not like the Japanese compacts Rusty's friends drove, where the horn beeped hello like a happy friend. The van honked. Like a goose on steroids. This did not have the desired effect. The car in front of Rusty sped up and the driver waved her fist in the mirror. Two gay men who had been strolling and holding hands gave the van the finger and conspicuously took down the licence number.

Sorry Vanwoman, thought Rusty. Now you'll be in the registry of gay bashers.

So much for Big J's Flowers. She had been going to circle the store until something happened, but instead she experimented with the power steering on some side streets. She sang along with Melissa. She wove in and out of traffic. She was a bit reckless and a lot of people got out of her way. It was fun. She decided to go out to Horseshoe Bay and eat fish and chips. Take a winding highway drive.

Rusty headed for the Lion's Gate Bridge in a rapid stream of traffic. Some cars seemed to be speeding down the wrong side of the street—wait, there was a little green arrow signal above their lane. Rusty didn't drive in Vancouver much, and she didn't like the look of this. She hugged the right-hand side of the road, as far away from the confusing arrow as possible. Which is how she ended up being sucked into Stanley Park in a right-turn-only lane that sprang up from nowhere. Sucked under a little bridge and into a slow-moving line of cars with out-of-province plates. Tourists.

They drove slowly because they were gawking at the ocean vistas and the mountain vistas and the huge trees. Rusty had to admit that Stanley Park was spectacular, vast and wild even on this road that circled its perimeter. You just knew there were wild things in there, in the dense trees. Like gay men. And gay bashers. Actually, Rusty had heard there were a lot of rabbits abandoned by Vancouver pet owners. Here on the outer fringes there were tour buses parked by the totems and by Lumberman's Arch, and a bezillion more at Prospect Point, their passengers staring at the wall of mountain and the bridge Rusty had been heading for before her traffic error.

She stopped at Third Beach when she realized it didn't matter whether she paid for parking. It wouldn't be Rusty who got the ticket. There are many benefits to a life of crime. She left the van and bought a hot dog, though she was too hyper to walk down the concrete stairs to the beach. She was sure that someone else would try to steal the van. She fingered the keys in her pocket nervously. She leaned against the wall of the snack bar while she ate, squinting.

She wished she had sunglasses.

She was on the lam, pumped up, trigger happy. Her accomplices Elzru and Brindlorava, swords by their sides, were counting money in the van. She wolfed down the hot dog like someone on the lam would. Gotta get to the next town, man.

As she pulled out of the parking lot, cops. Whoa, act normal, thought Rusty. What *is* the speed limit in Stanley Park? Really slow, anyway. But if she went too slow, they would think she was stoned and pull her over. Vanwoman must have reported the van by now, maybe the cops were already on the lookout. Maybe they were feeding the licence number into the computer to see if anything came up. Maybe those gay men had phoned her in.

Melissa Etheridge was driving her crazy.

Two Ends of Sleep

The cops followed her all the way through the park. One car passed, but the cops stuck to Rusty's tail and the other motorists stayed meekly behind. Rusty wondered if there was some ordinance that meant they couldn't arrest her in Stanley Park, that they were just waiting till she left the park to pull her over. Like maybe the park was federal land or something. Like maybe only the Mounties could bust her here. *Great*. Janet would know. Marooned in her stolen van, Rusty wanted Janet's brazen calm. If only she were here. But she wasn't.

Rusty figured she should stay in the park to be on the safe side. At Second Beach she took the turnoff to the lagoon. The cop car continued straight ahead. Her tension exploded loose in a hoot and a shiver—she was clear. And shaken. Phew. The steering wheel was slippery with sweat. She wiped her hands on her jeans. She checked the mirrors again. A car with Oregon plates was right behind.

"That's where the ducks are," she told them in her head. "The opening sequence of 'Danger Bay' was filmed there. You used to be able to rent those paddle boats but now there are too many people so they stopped." She realized then that she was talking out loud. Talking was soothing. Her voice hummed therapeutically in her throat, the sound was normal and immediate, like it was the most regular thing in the world for her to be driving some total stranger's van, which she had stolen, around Stanley Park.

"Nice van, eh?" she said. "I stole it. I'm a bit tired of Melissa Etheridge. Maybe I'll listen to the radio. Here's a good one. Classic rock. Chilliwack. 'Lonesome Mary' is the name of this one I believe." She cranked the Alpine. It was suited to this music. She sang along at the top of her lungs.

After one more trip around the park, Rusty was ready to

Two Ends of Sleep

leave. She had pointed out all the sights to the Oregonians, who remained behind her the whole way. "This is an enormous park that was logged when Vancouver was first taken over by white people. Here's a statue of Harry Jerome, famous Canadian athlete. Here's Prospect Point. Here's the Hollow Tree." On the way out she told them, "That's where they teach folk dancing in the summer. I went once with my girlfriend, Janet, when we started dating. It was really fun."

She had been driving for almost an hour. Vanwoman had missed her baseball game for sure. Rusty imagined the scene. The laundry is finally dry. Vanwoman unloads it into her bag in a huff and storms out without paying, only to discover the van is gone. Then she has to go back in and ask the woman she yelled at if she can please use the phone.

It is better to be the stealer than the stealee, no matter what they tell you.

Still, Rusty wanted to get home before Janet did, but she couldn't exactly pull up in the van. She was headed east and a strategy was needed. She had to ditch the van—but where? Obviously not at Laundr-Eeze, where the cops were no doubt already looking. Or if not the cops, Vanwoman.

Vanwoman's house! This was a stroke of genius. At a red light, Rusty leaned over and grabbed the insurance papers out of the glove compartment. Sure enough, there was an address for a Lesley A. Cressman. In Burnaby. Plus there was a map, which Rusty pulled over and studied. Vanwoman lived a little far away, but at least near a SkyTrain station. Rusty figured she had time to get there and back before Janet suspected anything was up.

"Coral!"

It took Rusty a minute to figure out what was happening. Someone was calling Vanwoman, who was apparently known as Coral. Therefore, someone was calling *her*—Rusty, Coral, Vanwoman, Lesley A. Cressman, whoever. It was like a play where Rusty had to remember her character's identity.

A woman was dashing across the street.

"I'd recognize that van anywhere!" she was saying as she drew near. Then, "Oh sorry," when she reached the door and saw Rusty. "I thought you were my friend Coral. This is her van, isn't it?"

She was looking in, staring at St. Christopher and Elzru. You bought them in stores, thought Rusty. Anyone could have them.

"It's my van," said Rusty defensively.

"Really? Amazing," said the woman. "Coral's van is, like, identical." She was standing very close to the window. Rusty turned so she blocked the woman's view of the inside.

"There's a few of them around," said Rusty.

"Yeah, I guess. But all those things—"

"I get it all the time," interrupted Rusty. "They're everywhere."

"I guess—." The woman didn't seem convinced.

"Look, I've got to go. Sorry," said Rusty. She drove off.

Close call.

She drove to Burnaby as fast as she could without attracting any cops. Vanwoman lived on a street of nondescript bungalows and three-storey apartments. Rusty parked a block away from where she figured the house was. She debated for some time whether she should leave the van unlocked with the keys on the seat like she found it, or lock the keys inside, which would be safer.

She locked it. Vanwoman must have a spare set, or an auto club to come and let her in.

Rusty walked away, caught the SkyTrain, strolled the few blocks home. Her heart was pounding. She sat in the kitchen, fidgeting. She was sure Janet would notice her nervousness and then ask questions. She thought frantically of things that casual people do—drink tea, cook dinner, read books.

When Janet arrived she was sitting in the living room with a novel and a steaming cup.

"Great, you're here, I'll put the quesadillas in the oven," she said cheerfully.

"You made dinner?" said Janet.

"I didn't have anything else to do, did I?" said Rusty.

Rusty didn't feel like phoning Dee very much after the dream about her and Eagle. She knew it was stupid, but she had been embarrassed in the dream and she was still embarrassed. Dee was toying with her. Except for that one phone call, she only heard from her if she wanted sex. So if Dee was more interested in Eagle just because Eagle had released a CD and met Courtney Love once, well Eagle could have Dee.

Rusty didn't believe that Eagle had really met Courtney Love anyway. She probably just went backstage with a big mob of fans.

And frankly, it had been fun to fuck Dee and everything, but just because she had MS didn't mean Rusty could lie around all day waiting for women to drop by with leaflets.

Rusty was busy. She was, after all, an auto thief.

Janet wanted to know about the Tai Chi.

"Did you ever get that number from Dee?"

"No."

"Why not?"

"I think Dee is a bit weird."

"Well, you don't have to marry her, you just have to phone her up and get that phone number. Tai Chi might be a good thing."

"Maybe."

"She's got some big exam soon and then she's leaving town, so do it soon."

Right, Dee was a professional or going to be.

"What is Dee, anyway?"

"She's going to be some kind of a therapist, I think. Some capital H Healing thing."

Dee? Therapist? She was so fucked up herself. She played games with people's minds, Rusty's mind in particular. She played women off against each other and used sex as a weapon. Rusty should be the therapist.

"I don't think I would go to her for therapy."

"No, me neither, but then again I don't think I would go to anyone for therapy, so it's kind of a dead-end discussion."

"We went to *Lesbians Loving* for therapy."

"And what a help that was."

Crash sent a fax. Rusty picked it up at the stationery store. It was a shitty day outside and she knew everyone at the store had read her fax, so she hoped it wasn't insulting.

It was very polite. It was mixed.

They wanted her article, but they didn't want the politics. They said they were "looking forward" to receiving her piece but added, "We are a non-partisan publication, and our readers have told us that they prefer it that way. We ask that our writers make every effort to maintain journalistic objectivity."

Bullshit, thought Rusty. She was euphoric, but pissed off. She considered her options.

Janet would never go for this. She would refuse to be interviewed. Dee would agree to be interviewed. Rusty was not sure if this was a good or a bad thing.

When she got home she phoned Janet, swallowed her pride, read her the fax.

"I told you," said Janet.

"I know," said Rusty. "Now what?"

"Why did you want to do this *Crash* thing anyway?"

Dee, thought Rusty. "My future," she said. "I don't want to just be a washed-up writer on welfare."

"There's nothing wrong with being on welfare. There's

nothing wrong with writing things you believe in. And you don't have to write anything if you don't want to."

"When did you turn into the Voice of Fucking Reason?" said Rusty.

The house across the street was a cipher. When she woke up, Rusty looked hopefully out the window, but the curtains were drawn, the door stayed closed. Two days in a row. Rusty worried they were gone. Maybe they moved because of the trees. Or maybe it was just too hard here in the city and they went to live in a small town. She should have shown them what nice neighbours you could have in the city. She should have gone over there and said hi.

"You know that house across the street?" she hazarded at dinner. They were eating late. It was dark, and no light had come on across the street.

"The trees?" said Janet.

"Exactly. The trees," said Rusty. "They're gone."

"What do you mean, they're gone? Of course they're gone, that's why we noticed the house."

"Not the trees, the people. The family is gone."

"Are you sure? I thought I saw those kids on Friday when I came home."

"They're gone now."

"You saw them move?"

"Well no, but no one has been there."

"They probably just went away for the weekend."

Rusty's life didn't include weekends. Her days rolled past,

same after same. Her life was either one long weekend or one long week, depending on how you looked at it.

Janet was right. Long after dinner, a car pulled up and idled outside the house while the woman got out and opened the front door, then ferried bags to the lit hallway. Then she carried the floppy sleeping children in, one by one. Rusty could see the child's head and the woman's back as she walked down the hall.

"Bye! Thanks!" the woman called from the door and closed it. The curtains glowed mutely. The car pulled away.

Rusty had never watched the house at night before.

Rusty was sitting by the computer, watching Janet type the minutes for her art action group.

"If I *do* do an article, who do you think I should talk to?" she asked.

Janet leaned back. "God, let's see. Minou knows the issues, but she's not one to talk about art. Talk to Kay if you want art jargon. Dee's a bit of an airhead—"

"I think Dee's an asshole," interrupted Rusty.

"Why?" said Janet

Rusty let that go.

"She means well," said Janet.

Rusty contemplated Janet's attempt at generosity. It reminded her of high school, girls gathered in the bathroom at lunch hour, putting on make-up while Rusty watched. In those days, they would say, "Not to be mean, but . . ." as a lead-in to small-spirited comments about sluttishness and fashion. Now, her friends said, "She means well," or worse still, "She's nice."

"She just gets really flaky and dogmatic when she's nervous. She's so shy and terrified of getting involved with anyone."

She sure wasn't shy about getting involved with me, thought Rusty. How did Janet know so much about Dee anyway?

"I guess you've been hanging around with her, what with the group and everything," said Rusty lamely.

"Yeah. She's okay. Better than hanging around with Kay, I can tell you that. Except she confides in me. Here's gossip for you. Dee has a crush on Lara and she doesn't know what to do."

The blow hit soundless in Rusty's chest. Lara? What about us? What about me? Would this never end? First Eagle, now Lara?

"Am I supposed to help?" she croaked. She felt herself dragged hapless in the current. Was she expected to arrange a blind date between her secret lover and her best friend?

"I don't think you *can* help. You know Lara. She'll string Dee along till Dee leaves town and then she'll forget all about it. I feel sorry for Dee, kind of. At this coffee thing last week, Lara was there and Dee went nuts on this other woman who was talking about installing an alarm at the Women's Bookstore. Get this, she had some crazy argument, like because the alarm notified the cops, it was dangerous since it let the State intrude on women's energy. Or something like that. No one got it really. Especially Lara. You should give Dee a break."

Give her a break? Because she's nice, maybe?

I'll give her a break, thought Rusty. I'll give her a break *from me* if she likes Lara so much.

Her own friend Lara. The "babe." Lock your door during your afternoon naps, Lara. Don't answer the phone during the day. Check your mailbox for perfumed letters.

"Despite being in a chair

and only being awake four hours a day, Louise is the emotional centre of her family."

Rusty reads this in one of the MS publications. They are full of the chirpy, happy people with MS who maintain the status quo against all odds. Women who crawl when they can't walk. Women who hike the Andes with their husbands. Women who nurture nurture nurture despite everything.

Rusty has never been a nurturer.

"Despite the fact that she sleeps all day, and when she's not sleeping, she's peeing, Rusty manages to do her feminist work, get her welfare stub in by the fifth of the month and still have time to go to dyke bars," jokes Janet. Rusty tries not to feel guilty, but it seems she will never heal herself at this rate.

Many days, she doesn't really want to heal herself. She does not want to lose the lapping sleep, the slow spiral down so many times a day, or lying eyes open while her body bends warm in the sun on the bed.

She likes welfare.

Rusty was waking up, still hovering in her dream, still not quite sure what time it was or what she should be doing. A waking state. A bell. It took a minute to register. Now what. Then a light tap tap tap. Ah, the door. Someone was using the knocker. Rusty knew what to do. She did up her pants. She went to the door.

It was Vanwoman.

Standing at the door with flowers in her hand. Behind her on the street was the van.

What the hell was *she* doing *here*?

"Hi," said Rusty before she remembered that she didn't know Vanwoman, had never seen her before in her life.

"Hello," said Vanwoman. "Is Janet home?"

"No," said Rusty. She felt like a cat. This is my territory so don't even think about it.

"Oh," said Vanwoman. "I brought her these flowers." There was an awkward pause. "My name's Coral." She was clutching the flowers. She blushed. "I mean, I know she works at a flower store and all and I, uh, thought she might be interested."

"Yeah, she might be," said Rusty. Not bloody likely.

"They're just from the corner store," said Coral. "I was in the neighbourhood and I—." Her speech trailed off. It is impossible to bring someone flowers and pretend you were just in the neighbourhood and just thought they might be interested because they're in the business. Flowers are flowers. Rusty let Coral sweat.

"Yeah, well, she's not home," she repeated.

"No," said Coral.

They looked at each other. Coral's eyebrow ring glistened. She scratched her neck.

"Could you, um, give them to her for me?" asked Coral finally.

"Okay," said Rusty.

"Just tell her they're from Coral. Oh, I said that. The woman with the van. I gave her a ride in my van once. She'll know who it is."

"Coral. I'll just write it down. How do you spell it?" asked Rusty. She walked back to the kitchen to get a pen. Coral followed with the flowers.

"C-o-r-a-l," said Coral. "Like a reef."

"Did you choose that name?" Did you choose that name, *Lesley*, added Rusty in her head.

"No. Everyone thinks so. I'm named after an aunt, actually."

An aunt? Then who the hell is Lesley Cressman? Maybe Coral was just another van thief.

"Can I use your washroom?" asked Coral.

"Fine. Down the hall," said Rusty. She lay the flowers on the counter with a note. "From Coral for Janet." Let Janet talk her way out of this one. She went back to wait by the door to show Coral out. There was the van, heartshaped window, mountain, desert, moons, right outside her house. She felt a certain proprietary interest. Had the tape selection improved? for instance. How were Elzru and Brindlorava doing? Had Coral cleaned up her beer cans?

"Nice van," she said when Coral came up beside her.

"Yeah, I guess."

"Must be great for camping," said Rusty.

"Yeah, it sleeps two."

"Lots of road trips, I suppose," said Rusty.

"Mostly I just take it to the bar," laughed Coral.

So I gather, thought Rusty.

"Did it cost a lot?" asked Rusty.

"Probably," said Coral. Probably? She *did* steal it. "It's not mine," she added. "It's my brother's. He's out of town."

What?

Rusty considered Coral's look—crewcut and pierced—and was forced to admit that the same aesthetic did not govern the mural. And what about the posters? Was Coral a fan of the medieval thing? Some lesbians were, even if they did have crewcuts. Whose posters were they? What about the Mores?

"Do you smoke Mores?" she asked.

"What?"

It had been a weird question. "Just wondering," Rusty trailed off.

"I don't smoke," said Coral.

"I mean, I see them all the time in stores, those skinny brown cigarettes, but I don't know anyone who smokes them, so I was just wondering, have you?"

Coral looked dubious.

"I'm doing a poll." Rusty looked serious, like she was doing a poll.

"My brother's girlfriend smokes them," said Coral.

"Oh wow, my first confirmed Mores smoker," said Rusty.

Her mind was not co-operating. The idea that the van—The Van—was actually owned by a straight guy in Burnaby sat naked in her head. And her mind was refusing to embrace it. No blanket of understanding was wrapping around it. The blanket of understanding lay very flat, and Rusty was being exposed to random, sharp realizations: that stealing Coral's van had been *très* stupid because it wasn't Coral's van anyway; that Coral's brother might press charges if he ever found out; that he wouldn't care about her being a dyke; that the street out in Burnaby was not Coral's street.

That Coral, in effect, remained a mystery, as did her relationship with Janet.

That Rusty had a felony to worry about now.

"Do you want to wait for Janet?" she asked Coral. "She should be home pretty soon." Rusty didn't want Coral to escape.

"Okay," said Coral. She looked a little stricken. Heartsick.

"I'll put the flowers in water," said Rusty.

"Thanks," said Coral.

"We can have tea, if you want." Rusty put water on.

"Okay," said Coral. "If you're making it anyway. I can just wait on the porch if you want though. I mean, I don't want to put you out or anything."

"It's fine," said Rusty. "Stay here in the kitchen." Coral was so polite. Rusty went and put on Melissa Etheridge, just to see Coral's reaction. Amateur detective. Maybe Coral would drop some information about Janet, stimulated by the music of their lovemaking.

"My brother loves Melissa Etheridge," said Coral when Rusty returned to the kitchen. "I swear that's why he thinks I'm okay, because Melissa's a dyke."

"Well that's handy."

"Yeah."

"Having a van like that must be great," said Rusty, trying another tack.

"Pros and cons."

"Yeah."

"It got stolen the other day."

"Really?"

"Yeah. I was getting my laundry. Just up here, actually. Boy do *they* give bad service. They were four hours late. Anyway, I'm sitting in the laundromat, waiting for my softball uniform so I can get to my game and I'm late already, and then when it's finally done, I go to leave and the van's gone!"

"Wow," said Rusty.

"It gets weirder. So I'm completely freaked out because my brother would kill me if I lost his van, and I had left it unlocked so he would really kill me. I was totally freaked out. I called the cops and they said they would keep an eye out for it, but since I left it unlocked it would be pretty hard to prove anything. And the insurance people weren't very helpful at all and oh man was I worried. Plus I missed my game of course. And I was stuck at that laundromat."

"Shit," said Rusty.

"I know. It was a huge drag. I had to call a cab to get home. Then later this friend of my brother's calls and he wants to know how come I brought the van back. What? I said. Well. Whoever stole the van dropped it off in front of his house, which is down the street from my brother's. They even locked it. So then I had to call a garage to get the keys out. Whoever stole it didn't take anything, either."

"Weird," said Rusty. The kettle was whistling, she poured the water.

"I'll say. Also this friend of mine swears she saw the van in

Two Ends of Sleep

the West End that afternoon with this kind of dykey woman behind the wheel. She talked to her and the woman acted nervous and drove away."

"Does she think she could recognize her?" asked Rusty. Shit.

"She says she could. I asked her to be on the lookout."

"Not much you could do, though," said Rusty, pouring the tea. Not much.

"No, not legally or anything. I could give her shit, though. And I could make sure other women knew what she was up to."

"Maybe she had a good reason," said Rusty. "For taking the van, I mean. Maybe it was an emergency."

"Maybe."

"She didn't wreck it."

"No."

"And she didn't take anything."

"No."

Rusty and Coral pondered the dyke villain. They sipped their tea.

There was noise on the porch.

"Here's Janet," said Rusty.

It wasn't Janet. It was Janet and Dee.

Janet stood still for a second at the door to the kitchen, looking at Rusty and Coral. Dee was behind her. Rusty winked. Dee gave her a weak smile. Chicken.

"Hi," said Coral. "Remember me?" Coral was looking very nervous. Janet was putting on a good act, but Rusty wasn't fooled.

"Coral brought you some flowers," said Rusty to Janet.

"I knew you worked at a flower store, so—," said Coral. She blushed again.

"Thanks," said Janet. She looked at the flowers. They included carnations, which Rusty knew Janet hated. Point for Rusty. "I didn't know you knew Rusty," she said to Coral. Haha, thought Rusty,

"I don't. We just met," said Coral.

"Yeah," said Rusty. "I'm Rusty."

"Coral gave me a ride once," said Janet to Rusty.

I know, thought Rusty, and that's not all. "So she said," said Rusty, looking at Janet. "I know all about the ride." That was a conversation stopper. The other three women looked at Rusty. Rusty looked at Dee and fingered her shirt buttons.

"Still got those posters?" said Janet to Coral.

"Unfortunately," said Coral.

"Coral's van has these posters," said Janet to Dee and Rusty, "of medieval warriors with the most enormous breasts."

"They're not *my* posters," said Coral. "They're my brother's."

Did Janet look tenderly at Coral?

"So what have you guys been talking about?" asked Janet.

"My van got stolen last week," said Coral.

"Oh," said Janet.

"We haven't been talking about the bar," said Rusty to Janet with a meaningful look. Janet looked at Coral.

"Really? Stolen?" said Dee. "What a drag." She moved into the room. She was ignoring Rusty. Very cool.

"I got it back," said Coral.

Rusty was trying to catch Dee's eye, but Dee was obviously really paranoid and refusing to engage.

"Her friend thinks she saw who stole it. A dyke," said Rusty recklessly.

"Our community is falling apart," said Dee. "This wouldn't

happen if lesbians didn't buy into traditional notions of success."

"It's her brother's van," said Janet irritably.

Rusty went into the living room and took off Melissa Etheridge. She put on the new CD that she and Dee had enjoyed together. Today she was using music as an investigative tool. When she got back to the kitchen, Janet was telling the other two about the CD, how they first heard it at Lara's. Dee was pretending to have never heard it before. Tricky.

"Well, thanks for the flowers, Coral," Janet said finally. "Maybe we should get together some time. Give me your number."

Like you don't have it already, thought Rusty. I've got your number.

"Don't you think this CD is beautiful?" she said seductively to Dee.

"Yeah, it's great," said Dee, cryptic as usual. "Lara has such great taste. I don't know where she finds out about these things."

"We've got work to do," said Janet. She turned to Coral. "We're working on a demo against the new immigration laws."

"Oh," said Coral. She had clearly never heard that there were new immigration laws. "Cool," she added. "Maybe I'll come." She was writing her phone number on the piece of paper that said "From Coral for Janet."

"Rusty's writing about the demo for *Crash*," said Dee.

Thank you. "Maybe," said Rusty modestly.

"We'll work in the other room," said Janet to Rusty.

"Oh," said Rusty. "Maybe I'll have a nap."

"I think everyone should nap regularly," said Dee. This must be my cue, thought Rusty. But for what?

"Well, you'd like Rusty," said Janet. "She's a regular napper."

"It's good to nap," said Rusty. "Sometimes people drop by."

"Really?" said Janet. "How do you know?"

"I hear them," said Rusty, looking pointedly at Dee. "More tea?" she said to Coral.

Coral looked confused. "I think I've gotta go," she said. She was still holding the paper with her phone number. She put it on the table and pushed it towards Janet. Janet put the scrap in her pocket.

"I've got ball practice," said Coral. She waved shyly at the room and walked down the hall. The front door opened and closed.

"Off to work," said Dee. She and Janet headed to the computer.

"Off to bed," said Rusty. She turned off the CD and lay on the bed, listening to Coral's brother's van leaving and the tapping keys in the next room.

Rusty saw the woman from the treeless house at the corner store. She was in line to pay for a bottle of pop and a bag of chips. The sproingy spring boy was doing his thing next to her.

"Hi," said Rusty. "Do you live in the house where the trees are gone?" As if she didn't know.

"Yeah," said the woman. "Are you a social worker or something?" She seemed a bit suspicious.

"Um, no. I'm not a social worker. I'm a writer, actually. I live across the street from you."

"Well, you can't interview me or anything."

"No, no. I just have a question. How come you cut down all those trees?"

"That wasn't me. You have to ask the landlord. He just came by one day and cut them all down."

"Why?"

"Who can say."

Rusty couldn't think of anything else.

"See you around!" she tried hopefully.

"Yeah," said the woman.

"Yeah yeah yeah," said the boy, bouncing a few times.

Rusty was up at seven, anxious about her *Crash* article or at least about whether there would be one. There was still time to say she wouldn't do it and still time to say she would. She lay in bed and listened to Janet getting ready for work: shower, dresser drawers, toaster, fridge door, dishes in sink, key in lock.

Key in lock.

At nine she phoned the flower store.

BJ was on her way to some hearing about Rusty's insurance-coverage case, Janet said.

"Thanks," said Rusty. "Do you always lock the door when you leave?"

"Yeah, why? What's wrong with that? You're always asleep, anything could happen. Why? Should I stop?"

"No, it's fine, I'm glad you lock the door."

Well, that threw in a whole new twist.

Rusty called Dee. It wasn't very hard to do. She just wore the same outfit she had been wearing all day.

"Hi, it's Rusty. I just called to see if you have that Tai Chi number."

"Wait a minute, my place is such a mess, studying, packing. Here it is." Dee had never even had a flyer. Rusty knew that now.

"Well, let us know if you need any help with your move. I'm not very strong, but I can do other things. Phone places or something."

"Hey, thanks. How are you at packing? I thought I might call Lara and some other people too. Just call Lara up and see if she can help. I don't believe in paying movers to do what we can do as a community, you know?"

Well, no, thought Rusty, I don't know. I do know that I have never been having an affair with you. I imagined it.

Rusty's imagination was free-wheeling, slipping easily through worlds of sleep and waking, pulling threads together and weaving lustrous stories.

What else in her life was a fiction? she wondered.

Rusty was writing to *Crash*.

"Fuck you," said her letter. She deleted that. She also deleted, "What's wrong, scared of lesbians?"

Instead she wrote, "Thank you for your fax of last week and for your interest in my work. Regrettably, the editorial constraints you have imposed on my writing make it impossible for me to submit my piece to *Crash* at this time."

Fair enough.

She faxed it.

She went back to bed.

The secret to a peaceful life is to first create a difficult one. Now there was a clean space where *Crash* had been, and Rusty needed the sleep.

"What happened to Dorothy Parker?" asked Janet.

"Dorothy lives," said Rusty.

Rusty looks at people on scooters

and thinks, if *they're* here, then this is a place I would be able to go. She looks to see how many of them are using Scampers. Some.

Probably the same proportion of people name their scooters as name their cars. Too many, in Rusty's opinion, but it can't be helped.

People using scooters do not have a monopoly on cheesy bumper stickers, she reminds herself. Nor do people with MS have a monopoly on sentimental aphorisms. Look at AA, for god's sake.

Rusty hears about a disability activist. She has no arms and wears formfitting leather when she sits above the lectern, turning pages with her feet.

Rusty, being a lesbian, is a bit tired of leather outfits, but she likes the idea. She thinks about the artist Frida Kahlo in her hospital bed, making surreal paintings on her full body cast. Rusty wants a sleeping place that is an art piece. She wants her bed to belong to more than her imagination. She wants more than imaginary affairs, more than intensity without substance.

She wants she wants for the first time in a long time.

"I don't want to waste my research," said Rusty to Janet about the *Crash* article fiasco. "I mean, maybe I should write something anyway. *Insister* needs help in the arts coverage department. I could write for them."

"Okay," said Janet.

"Don't be so enthusiastic," said Rusty.

"I don't want to suggest something and then have you tell me I'm insensitive to your fatigue," said Janet.

"Okay," said Rusty. There was nowhere to go in that argument. "Do you think your group will mind?"

"No one but Kay. I think she's already put your *Crash* article into the 'Reviews' part of her CV. I don't think they read *Insister* at the Canada Council."

"They should," said Rusty. "What about Dee?" It was a reflex.

"What about her? She's leaving town anyway. What does she care?"

"Okay, *Insister* it is," said Rusty.

Janet came home early from work one day and nudged Rusty awake. When Rusty opened her eyes, Janet kissed her all over her face and neck.

"Kissing is best," she said.

Rusty was hardly awake. Janet's mouth was hard on hers. It was enticing, so intense.

"Give me a minute," said Rusty. "Tell me a story or something."

"I'll tell you a fantasy," said Janet, lying down next to Rusty. "One of my fantasies. In it I've got this really fancy car."

"A van?" said Rusty.

"No, more like a limo. With a chauffeur. I get the chauffeur to take me to the bar and then wait outside." Janet put her fingers in Rusty's mouth and moved them around slowly. "And in the bar I pick up women and then I take them outside and fuck them in the limo."

"Does the chauffeur watch?" asked Rusty. Janet's fingers were tracing the line of her shirt, her breasts, her waist.

"Oh yes, and sometimes the women know he's watching and sometimes they don't." Janet was moving her whole body down, moving her head to Rusty's cunt.

"Do the women like it?"

"They love it," said Janet, undoing Rusty's pants. "They

know who I am and they all want to come with me. Sometimes I have to bring two of them at once. I'm there all night, fucking women at the bar. I just go in and stand by the dance floor and someone asks me to dance, and then I ask them to come outside."

"Am I there?" asked Rusty. Janet was pulling Rusty's pants off.

"Sometimes. Sometimes I let you go in and pick the women for me, and then I make you sit in the front with the chauffeur while I fuck them."

"I don't want to sit in the front right now," said Rusty.

"No, I don't want you to either," said Janet and began licking. Rusty's body spiralled out of itself.

Rusty slept all day sometimes. Sometimes all day and all night, dreaming.

On the Drive, Rusty saw the wires above her head in the clear sky, smooth black lines. She saw the tiniest bits of weeds growing in cracks. At night she saw the roadway glistening after the rain, pieces of garbage pinned in the light. Watched teenagers posture around the phone booth.

"I thought you had left town," said the editor of *Insister* when she called. "Will you have any pictures we can use? I'm putting you next to the news about the farmworkers' strike."

One day Rusty looked out the window and saw the little spring fighting with the girl over the board/chainsaw. Saw Janet in the distance on her way home.

Another day, BJ phoned and said, "Do you want to read some of the documentation we have gathered on MS patients and life insurance?"

"No," said Rusty.

She had broken her toe, tripping on her way to the phone.

Rusty and Janet drove Dee to the airport in Lara's car. Lara was supposed to go too, but something came up. Standing at the gate, watching Dee pass through security, Rusty felt it, the tug of her cuteness. She kind of wanted to follow her all over again. Dee turned, waved. She stuck her finger in her mouth and winked.

Bye, thought Rusty. What the fuck was that about?

Janet grabbed her arm. "I have the afternoon off now."

"Just wait," said Rusty, "I have to pee."

She walked the long hall to the bathroom. People were coming and going around her. Leaving on big trips. Parting and uniting. Dragging suitcase dogs behind them, and wheeling huge stacks of matched luggage. It all seemed festive. Rusty felt good.

In the bathroom everything was more than clean: sinks, counters, hand dryers, stainless (and they were) steel paper towel dispensers. Rusty felt underdressed. The stall was clean, too. Only one brave traveller had used a ballpoint pen to write anything: "I am leaving my life."

Heavy.

Rusty knew better. She took out a pen and wrote "Pee here now."

"I stole Coral's van," said Rusty. They were on their way home from the airport.

"What?"

"It was me," said Rusty. "I stole her van."

"Really?"

"Yeah." Rusty was acting cool.

"Why?"

"No reason. I just took it."

"You do this all the time?" asked Janet.

"No, only that one time."

Janet laughed. "Let me get this straight. You broke into Coral's van and stole it. For no reason. You just felt like it."

"It was unlocked. I didn't have to break in."

"Why were you even trying the door?" This was getting more complicated than Rusty had anticipated.

"I was looking in the window," she said.

Janet seemed to think this was hilarious. "Do you just walk up to random cars in the street and look in the window and then try the door?"

"Only Coral's, and only that one time."

"I get it," said Janet slowly. "Do you have a thing for Coral? Is that why she came by for tea?"

"You're the one with the thing for Coral."

"Are you crazy?"

"No."

"I don't have a thing for Coral. She just gave me a ride one night, Rusty. The night we had a fight and I went to the bar by myself."

"I know she did. I saw her drop you off," said Rusty victoriously. It was her trump card.

"And that's why you stole her van?" asked Janet.

It sounded stupid now.

"And now her friend who saw me is going to recognize me and I'm going to be drummed out of the community."

Janet was laughing again. "My little criminal. Don't worry, Rusty. We'll deny the whole thing. Why would you have stolen Coral's van? We'll tell them it's a case of mistaken identity. Or do you want to leave the country?"

"You think I'll be okay?"

"Yes, you'll be okay. We won't tell anybody else. And any other time you're jealous, you just go right ahead and steal a vehicle, Rusty. It impresses me. We could be a team. I'll cruise women with Jaguars and Mercedes Benzes, and then you'll steal their cars." She was still laughing. "How far did you go in the van anyway?"

"Not far. How far did *you* go?"

"I told you. Home."

"I went to Stanley Park."

"Good plan."

"I didn't wreck it or steal anything."

"No."

"You don't think I'm an asshole?" asked Rusty.

"I don't think you're an asshole, I think you're a lunatic." Janet smiled. She took one hand off the steering wheel and squeezed Rusty's knee.

With the curtains closed the room had a dim light, blurry and serene. Rusty lay on her side and closed her eyes to watch the day unfold, at first insistent and crowded, then in wisps. Rusty knew the way to sleep, how the brassy waking hours need to be counted before they could dissolve and uncover the rippling landscape beneath.

There was a blissful period when she didn't know whether she was awake or asleep. It was the moment when she knew the path before her was almost revealed, that she would certainly be pulled along. There were hovering cartoon fragments of wakefulness, and her own lingering attempts to understand them. And the familiar bright pushing shapes.

Then an unaccountable river of dreams.

ACKNOWLEDGEMENTS

The following people helped make this book possible. All the shortcomings are, of course, my own.

Persimmon Blackbridge had more to do with the creation of this book (and with boosting my confidence) than anyone else, proving that two people can a writer's group make.

Nancy Pollak was everything I hoped for in an editor: politically astute, meticulous and funny.

Press Gang Publishers has the mysterious alchemy that turns inspiration into books. My thanks go to everyone there: Barbara Kuhne, for putting the idea in my head in the first place, as well as much subsequent help; Della McCreary, for keeping Press Gang going and making sure people hear about our books; Val Speidel, for beautiful design.

I first wrote this as part of the International 3-Day Novel Competition, an experience I heartily recommend. Thanks go to Brian Kaufman, who assured me it would be worth it, and to Anvil Press, which organizes the event.

Rachel Rocco read the very first draft halfway through the weekend, and her comments about sex fantasies are with me still.

My experiences with Persimmon Blackbridge and Susan Stewart in Kiss & Tell have been pivotal in many ways—from writing about sex to thinking about my place as a lesbian in the world.

My friends will know this is not autobiography because Marlon and Jeseka Hickey make no appearance on these pages. The novel about lesbian mothers will have to wait. I am grateful to Marlon and Jeseka for their tolerance of my crankiness, for providing a window to contemporary pop culture, and for being willing to read lesbian fiction in between bouts of *PC Computer* and *Archie* comics.

Suzo Hickey was a tireless advocate for Janet. Plus she was encouraging, attentive, funny and unfailingly supportive. We'll both be getting much-needed sleep soon.

ABOUT THE AUTHOR

Lizard Jones is a writer, visual artist and performer who is involved in social activism and the alternative media and has a penchant for working collaboratively. Her work as a member of the lesbian art collective Kiss & Tell has been exhibited in Canada, the U.S., Hong Kong, Australia and Europe. She is co-author of the Lambda Award-winning *Her Tongue on My Theory*, and of *Drawing the Line: Lesbian Sexual Politics on the Wall*. Her writing and artwork have been widely published in journals and in the anthologies *Forbidden Passages; Tangled Sheets;* and *Nothing But the Girl*. As well, articles and reviews have appeared in *Fuse, Video Guide, Kinesis, Parallelogramme* and *Herizons*, among others.

Raised in Toronto and Calgary, Lizard Jones graduated from Princeton University and now lives in Vancouver. She was diagnosed with Multiple Sclerosis in 1994.

An earlier version of *Two Ends of Sleep* won Honourable Mention in the 1995 International 3-Day Novel Competition and an excerpt from it was published in *sub-TERRAIN* magazine.

Press Gang Publishers has been producing vital and provocative books by women since 1975. Visit us online at:

> http://www.pressgang.bc.ca

A free catalogue of our books in print is available from:

> Press Gang Publishers
> #101-225 East 17th Avenue
> Vancouver, B.C. V5V 1A6
> Canada